Praise for

SEPULCHRE

"Lon has captured teenage angst in the small town world of Dairy Queens and corner hardware stores. I devoured the story and finished the book in a few short hours. A quick read that stays with you. And a brutally honest portrayal of sexual slavery that goes on in the land of the "free." A convincing portrayal of the loss and anger of a parent who has no closure, and that loss of innocence, family and ultimately hope. Readers will be spurred on to help the Ambers and Rays of the world escape the 'sepulchre of death.'"

—Gail Weinhold
Assistant Professor of English
North Central University, Minneapolis, MN

"Lon Flippo has vividly described the dark torment sex trafficking inflicts on its victims, but also the incredible light and healing faith can bestow. The message is artfully entwined with a suspenseful, emotionally gripping and engrossing fictional tale of a man's unshakeable love for his lost daughter."

—Neil Dunlop
Journalist, editor

Also by Lon W. Flippo

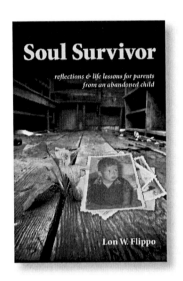

SEPULCHRE

SEPULCHRE

†

LON W. FLIPPO

CHRISTIAN LIFE PUBLISHERS
Columbus, Georgia

Printed in the United States of America

19 18 17 16 15   1 2 3 4 5

ISBN 978-0-9904452-3-4

Designed by Dawn M. Brandon

For my daughter Ashley.
I love you always.

1

Amber's fingers fumbled for the zipper on her jacket as the cold wind bit at her exposed skin. She tugged the short skirt down and fought onward.

Her red lips nearly numb, she mumbled the words of the song tumbling through her mind. The clipped phrases, meaningless to some, were truth to Amber, for they described her daily life.

I walk this street of broken dreams. I walk alone.

It was another bitter day. Just like yesterday. Nothing special. Nothing new. Her eyes darted for cues, searching for the man who'd bring her next fix or subsequent trick. One part focused on the necessities of her existence, the other scanning for a savior. A savior who might come and take her out of this desperate survival free from more bumps, bruises and battles.

Without warning, a blast of icy wind chilled her to the bone and she slipped into a nearby alcove off the sidewalk to escape.

The sign read "CLOSED" as Amber stamped and cupped her frigid hands, peering into the abandoned shop. Through the dirty window she glimpsed trash, shards of glass and pieces of old furnishings. A small gray mouse darted across the dusty floor.

Startled, she gasped, and shivering, pulled back from the plate glass. She hated mice. They ran across her floor at night and frightened her to immobility. Regaining her sense of urgent need, she shuffled back to the street.

The city was deserted. *What was she doing out here?*

Through her open-toed high heel (the warmest pair she owned) she felt something brush her foot and glancing down, she spied a small paperback book. Upon closer inspection it had no cover or title page, only a blank black cover, seemingly beckoning to be examined. She would investigate later tonight after supper.

She placed it in her small shoulder pack. It might be a delicious mystery to devour under the covers. Or maybe a zombie thriller or a sci-fi adventure. She wouldn't ruin the surprise now, but instead resumed her slow walk across the forsaken wasteland of inner-city Chicago, her heart and soul as abandoned as the old shop she compelled herself to push away now, along with all the memories and fragments of days long past.

She burst into her father's dingy store, the bell on the door clattering. Ray's Hardware was the best hardware store in Gilroy, maybe even in all of western Kansas, though she'd never traveled any further. As the youngest of three children living on a farm with her father, mother, and Uncle Arthur, she'd had her run of the huge house, and while her family was loving and kind, they had their share of drama and troubles. Her mother managed the house, her dad's brother Arthur supervised the farm, and her father ran the store.

"Somebody has to pay the bills," her dad always said, and off to town he meandered to tend the shop. He hadn't seemed unhappy, but he never did talk much beyond tools and sports.

"Can I come to town with you, Daddy, please?" she'd asked him that day. It was her favorite mantra and she knew he grew tired of the daily begging. Yet he easily gave in to her, his baby, and her promises of "helping out" at the store.

The truth was, Amber had been Ray's hidden personality disorder. And though she suspected it in later years, she'd never known how no matter what he'd tried, he couldn't seem to help spoiling his youngest. He doted, coddled and pampered his "Amber-lamb." Unexplainable even to himself, his wife Amanda had often bristled at his treatment of her.

Amber had loved the bins of screws, bolts, hammers, and pliers. She played hard and worked little. But neither of them cared. Ray loved her. Her warmth and silliness brightened his daily routine. And Amber enjoyed her freedom.

Hour after hour, day after day, she wiled away many a moment playing in the back room or running the aisles of the crowded store.

"Be careful Amber-lamb" her daddy would yell.

"I am, Daddy, I am!"

———

Like most fourteen-year-olds Amber wanted attention, she no longer wanted to play in the back room or run the crowded aisles of her daddy's store. All she craved, all she wanted was to be noticed. That, and to have fun. Lots of fun.

Inquisitive and precocious, she became a bossy, agitated teen-ager. Soon Amber insisted on hanging out with her friends during the long, hot summer days and though Amanda warned and chided him, Ray continued to give in to her. And despite the gift, Amber had made sure her dad knew her thoughts on the matter.

"Daddy, I'm going out with Meghan and Sarah. I'm outta this dump!" She flipped her long hair as she sauntered out the front door.

"Check in for lunch or you'll be grounded," Ray said, attempting to set some parental boundaries.

"Fine, Dad," Amber sighed.

Of course she didn't check in. Amber passed the hours swimming with her friends at the local park and eating cheap candy and greasy burgers.

It struck her now as nearly impossible but she'd hated the farm. She refused to spend one extra moment in that drab old house with its musty smell and creaky floors. She knew her family loved her but they didn't understand her. They didn't think like she did. Didn't like the music she liked and didn't even pretend to understand her world.

Why wouldn't they even try?

The only one who came close was Daddy. And only in rare moments. Most of the time he was lost in a fog of paperwork, a pile of boxes or a flurry of customers constantly streaming in and out.

In Amber's mind they'd resembled the little red ants scuttling beneath the old oak tree in the south pasture. The people pushed open the scratched plate glass door marching in and out, always busy and always seemingly angry about something broken. So stuck and ignorant in their puny little lives. At age fourteen, Amber was already determined to know more of life than this little pitiful town could ever conceive of.

4

Still, town was more palatable than the farm. Farm work was hideous, and any person would hate it, let alone a pretty, vivacious fourteen-year-old.

Sarah and Meghan were her best friends. Together they walked, talked, swam, and snacked the hours away. Her father continually demanded an appearance at the shop for lunch and arrival was expected promptly at 5:00 PM for the tedious ride back to the farm. And mostly, she complied.

But it was about two o'clock on a July afternoon as Amber, Sarah, and Meghan meandered down Walnut Street that freedom suddenly rolled up. Strolling their way to the park, a beautiful red Chevy Impala quietly pulled up beside them.

"Hey, girls. It's sure hot," the driver drawled.

"Hey yourself!" Amber drawled back, acting brave.

"Who are you?" Meghan asked.

"Johnnie."

"You're new here," Amber realized as the words slipped out she just revealed she knew all the boys in town.

"I am. And I just happen to be visiting cousins over in Wellsville and thought I'd get some ice cream at the Dairy Queen. Know where it is?"

"Amber," Sarah tugged at Amber's arm, trying to get her to ignore him and walk faster.

Amber patted Sarah's arm and smiled at Meghan. "You buying?"

"Sure I will!" Then, seeming to catch himself, he continued, "I mean, I'd love to. Y'all are the three prettiest girls this side of the Mississippi." His drawl was like those Texas outlaws in the movies, and his eyes twinkled catching the bright Kansas sun.

Meghan and Amber laughed. Sarah continued her death grip on Amber's arm.

"My treat!" He said.

"How old are you?" asked Amber.

"Seventeen. How old are you?"

His blue eyes took them in, up and down.

"Amber!" Sarah whispered a little too loudly.

"Amber," Johnnie repeated thoughtfully and a strange feeling had gripped her as he breathed her name again. His tight shirt revealed bulging muscles and his dark wavy hair was like a film star's.

Dropping Sarah's arm like a sack of nails, Amber and Meghan ambled over to the passenger-side window.

"Sounds yummy," cooed Amber while Meghan giggled once again.

"Jump in and I'll drive us over."

Amber stood up, warning bells blaring in her head. But this slightly-goofy, incredibly good-looking boy was like something straight out of a romance novel. Glancing back at Sarah's stunned look, she flipped her hair and said, "Sure."

Surprised but smiling, Meghan nodded and moved toward the car.

Meghan and Amber simultaneously reached for the door handle anxious to climb in, both fighting for the chance to sit in the front seat.

Sarah sputtered. "I . . . can't. I have to ask my mom."

"Come on, Sarah," Amber and Meghan droned.

She blinked and slowly climbed in after them.

Johnnie was kind, the ice cream was good, and later Amber rushed into the store eager to tell her father all about it. Part of her knew he wouldn't be as excited about it as she was, but Ray's reply was even more shocking than she'd expected. Ray had threatened her with grounding for the rest of the summer if she ever did something like that again.

"Amber, he's a stranger. You've known better since preschool. This is not a safe idea for you."

"Daddy, you don't understand."

"Let me tell you something, Amber. There's only one thing a seventeen-year-old boy wants from a pretty girl."

"Daddy, there were three of us. We were safe. I know it."

Ray's eyes met Amber's and the look silenced her. What came from his mouth next had haunted her for nearly a decade.

"You know nothing. Stay away from him, Amber, or I'll never bring you to town again. He's trouble. I mean it."

She was surprised and a little scared at the low tone in his voice. "Yes, Father." She'd forced out the syllables. Her lips moved like an old silent movie or a bad lip sync. Words from her mouth but absent of heart.

He had won her agreement but he'd lost *her*.

———

She'd forgotten most of the other details. Only splashes of memories now, bursts of feelings floating through her mind, and she fighting alternately to refresh and forget the distant events of that day. Like forgotten pennies on the dresser, she'd long pretended they didn't matter. She denied their place in her history but she knew in the pit of her stomach, in the hollow of her mind, the truth about her past would never, ever be completely forgotten.

It was a Tuesday, Amber recalled, and she had swimming lessons later at the city pool. Only eleven o'clock in the morning, and already the girls felt the boredom burrowing into them. Walking through the quiet streets and idly talking about the latest YouTube video, it wasn't enough to distract from the all-too-familiar hot day. It was never enough.

7

Johnnie had pulled up right after lunch.

"Hey, you girls want to do something special?"

Like a fly to flypaper, Amber's mind circled that moment in time.

"Of course!" Meghan laughed and Amber nodded, hardly remembering her promise to her father.

"Get in," Johnnie said. "Let's go for a ride."

Amber and Meghan quickly jumped into the front seat while Sarah again replied, "I'd better ask my mom."

"Come on!" they said.

"It'll be fun."

"No, I can't."

"Sarah," Meghan had whined.

"Go ahead," said Johnnie. "We'll come back and pick you up in a few minutes."

She'd watched Sarah through the window as the car pulled away in a cloud of dust; the wind lifting their hair into their faces as they drove off, waving goodbye.

2

Amber thumbed the dial of the radio searching for a top forty song as they flew down the road. Meghan laughed as the wind blew their hair across their faces. The music blared and Johnnie flashed his smile at them.

Fifteen minutes later Johnnie slowed the car and turned down a dirt road.

"Where we going, Johnnie?" Amber asked.

"Someplace special. It's right down this road." Smiling at Amber once more, he added, "You girls sure look pretty today."

Something in the way he said it had caused Amber's suspicions to mount. Looking at Meghan she knew they both felt the same. Something was different. Terribly, horribly changed. Teasing a second glance at her, Amber saw it clearly in his face this time: a crooked, almost devilish grin on his mouth. His eyes fastened on her like he no longer inhabited his own skin, and Amber felt her heart pounding, a ball of fear beginning to build in her gut.

Did I make a mistake? she wondered. How bad was this going to be? What was the worst that could happen?

Get out! part of her screamed.

Don't ruin it. He likes you. He's a nice guy.

"Hey, you girls okay?" Johnnie asked.

No, Amber thought. *We're dead.*

"Yes," she mumbled. "Fine."

"Cool." Johnnie gazed again at Amber and another huge grin crossed his face. "For a second there I thought you looked scared. And Johnnie doesn't want that."

He couldn't be bad, she thought.

But right now, standing in another forgotten doorway on a filthy street in downtown Chicago, she knew how wrong she'd been.

On warm nights, Amber would sometimes make soap bubbles with her brother and sister. They'd throw out the bubble wands that came inside and use their own. Those cheap plastic wands would bend and the bubbles would pop instead of expanding and growing strong.

She'd opened her mouth to say, "Turn this car around right now, Johnnie, and take us home." But instead, she bent and heard herself say, "Ohh, look at that beautiful horse."

On either side of the lane, perfectly painted white fence posts held the most beautiful horses Amber and Meghan had ever seen. And soon, Johnnie turned the car toward an old barn which rose majestically at the end of the drive. Johnnie slowed the car, killed the engine and parked.

"Wait here. It's a surprise," he said.

Meghan turned to her. "Are we going to ride them?" She shouted after him. "Please? Oh my gosh." She squealed with delight.

"Just wait here. I need to get permission." Johnnie headed off and then stopped and returned. "You'll need these wristbands." He handed them two black plastic zip-ties. "So they know you're here to ride." He glanced back at the girls and gave a slight hand wave and disappeared into the barn.

"What?" Amber looked at them. Meghan shrugged.

Moments later, two big men appeared and walked quickly to the car. They weren't talking and looked nervous. One looked around, his face flushed. The older, uglier one tore open the passenger door of the car and instantly, a switch was tripped and understanding settled on the girls.

"Oh no, Amber," Meghan whispered.

"Be quiet," Amber said.

"Hands," the man said. The girls didn't move. "I said, show me your hands."

Meghan looked ready to cry but she held her hands out. Amber held up hers.

"Where're your bands?" the other man asked loudly.

"Out," the older man said and the girls quietly stepped out.

"Put 'em on," the younger man gestured to the zip-ties in Amber's hand.

"Why?" Amber said, facing him and hearing her heart in her ears.

His eyes scanned them. "Oh, you want me to do it?"

"Just do it, Amber," Meghan said, taking one from her and snapping it on her wrist.

"Pretty," the older man said and he smiled slightly at Amber.

"They'll do," said the younger, "Listen, I'll do it if you don't want to."

Amber complied and the plastic teeth clicked through the little square opening.

11

Just then, Johnnie exited the barn folding an envelope into his jeans.

"Good work," grinned the younger of the men. "Now go find a couple more."

"But not in that town again," the older one said.

"Obviously," Johnnie sneered.

"Try the Salina truck stop. Lots of runaways there," the other man added shaking his shoulders in a strange dance Amber remembered looking more like a convulsion.

"Johnnie," Amber said. She wanted any sign to show he cared, but casting one final look into his blue fire eyes, she felt struck across the face. It had been her first lesson in betrayal, and of the many to follow, it had hurt the worst.

It was that look that convinced her to accept she would forever be abandoned.

"Enjoy the ride, girls," he said and hopped in the car. He fired it up.

"Hey, where's the ether?" the older man yelled at him.

"No. NO!!" Amber screamed and the older man suddenly grabbed her. She could see Meghan out of the corner of her eye struggling against the younger man who had grabbed her from behind. They fought and kicked hard, but the men only squeezed harder. The older one cursed.

"Don't you want that ride?" the younger man wheezed. "Better calm down!"

Watching the dust billow into crimson streaked sky, Amber turned slowly to watch the car flashing away and in that moment she knew: she was in serious trouble. It was the moment of her life she would never forget. Childhood was gone like the last gasping breath of air before going down, that final day of summer.

She brought her foot down hard and then suddenly she was free and she began to run. As if chasing Johnnie's car would somehow restore the beauty, the wonder of the world before the sun set on her dreams. But how could it have mattered?

Running as fast as her feet could fly, forgetting Meghan, forgetting everything, her one thought, her only purpose for existence now, was escape.

"Come back here you little piece of . . ."

The wind whipped through her ears drowning out the sound, but Amber ignored the voice and willed her body to fly. Step by step she raced the horses behind the fence, down the road toward her freedom, fighting off the dust lingering in the sunlight.

She was going to make it.

Suddenly she remembered Meghan and instantly the back of her head exploded into tiny fragments of light. And the horses ran.

She hoped she was dead. But her lips tasted dirt and blood and her face was smashed into the ground.

He was on top of her in the empty ditch.

"Don't ever run from me, girl," the older ugly man panted in her ear.

"I'll teach you."

Face down, her arms and legs pinned by the weight of his body, he cinched another ziptie to her wrist binding her hands together, and quickly ripped her cotton shorts from her body. Screams tried to escape her throat but they stifled in the pressure forcing out her own breath. The violation was an uglier thing than she'd ever imagined.

———

Strangely, she didn't cry once, not all that endless day. But later that night, tied and gagged in the trunk of an old car, she cried. She cried to know Meghan was gone and as the tires hummed angrily and the realization that she was stolen sank deeply into her mind. The life she once knew was gone, no more than some wasted milk poured out on the ground. When they stopped, she overheard the man say "Chicago" just before the trunk opened and the smelly rag was placed over her face again. She embraced the darkness, hoping against hope for death. That drugged state would be her cheapest ally in the long, hot hours before her. A voyage changing her life forever. A passage skipping adolescence and marching her straight into an abyss of a broken existence.

Amber emerged from her reverie. She realized she was shivering. She wondered if the tremors were the cold or need for her next stimulant. Broken, dirty and abandoned, the shop was her pitiful life. Consuming and being consumed had become her way of life. She'd had no idea how strong her will to survive was until it was bound into submission. Facing the intolerable, the human will either rises to fight or is squashed like a bug on the pavement. Former cares like watching your favorite television show or what clothes to wear fade in the encroaching darkness of insanity once safety is no longer an option. What remained for Amber was a driving whispered urge to embrace her longings for food, drugs, money and survival.

A remnant of a long-forgotten high-school English class forced its way into her memory, a memorized poem by Edgar Allen Poe.

> *In the sepulchre, in her tomb.*
> *And so, all the night-tide, I lie down by the side*
> *Of my darling—my darling—my life and my bride,*
> *In her sepulchre there by the sea—*
> *In her tomb by the sounding sea.*

Someone had asked what a sepulchre was—a small room or crypt carved out of stone where the dead could be laid.

In the glass' reflection, she could see she was trapped, the walls high and tight around her.

My life is a living tomb, she thought. *A sepulchre.*

She'd awoken startled the night they'd brought her to Chicago, her first night in the tiny room alone. Glancing around the darkened space, she saw nothing. A strange snapping sound fired in her ears.

Snap-snap . . .

Silence.

Snap-snap . . .

It continued and the room soon seemed to thunder with the noise. In terror, she whipped her head about frantically searching for it. *Snap . . . Snap . . .* Deep and sustained, it reverberated through the tiny space and pounded into her skull. At times, it came in rapid fire, one after the other. But most often in sequences of two.

Snap-snap . . .

Snap . . .

Amber covered her head, and shut her eyes against the dark, but even there, the sound continued. She dove back into the tousled sheets and buried her weak body deep, cold and longing for safety.

Her breath was shallow and the damp room seemed to soak in all other sound. She lay perfectly still, making no sound and waiting for the eerie noise to return. But it didn't come. Only the air escaping her nostrils and the faint buzz of the electric alarm clock. Then, without warning—

Snap-snap.

She jumped.

Then once more.

Snap-snap.

Terror gripped her as though the sound was the embodiment of all the evil she'd recently witnessed, and hot tears slid down her face.

A new awareness was dawning upon her, distinct and deep. A knowledge she would carry with her for years.

For the first time in her life she understood the true meaning of *fear.*

Slithering down her hair, descending to her back and creeping along her arms and legs even under her toenails, she might have called it a demon. But she had never been told what a demon was let alone what it felt like. But for now, this partial understanding was what she had.

Fear not only had a presence, it had a sound.

It crept into her and strangled every shred of life and peace out of her.

That night would come to be known as the night Amber had died.

———

The transformation had been quick though not painless. They changed her makeup and dyed her black hair blonde. She was shaved, waxed and finally, given the tattoo of a rose on the small of her back.

He'd named her Misty.

Imprisoned in a room of four windowless walls, her only companion was a tiny television. Alone, she waited until the door was unlocked and a man would walk in. Hour after hour, day after day. The endless terror had wound itself around her spirit like a giant leech, sucking the life from her soul.

The emptiness of her space made her confinement pure misery. Without any possessions upon her arrival, she was broken of any sense that she could own, let alone deserve even simple objects. Eventually, she learned to get things from the men who were kinder than the rest, things fitting for a teenage girl: a hairbrush, makeup, a few clothes—stuffed animals. The toys always seemed out of place, but she welcomed them. Clutching a red teddy bear and a white unicorn fiercely each night, they were her only solace, though insufficient.

"Guess we do have to keep you purty," muttered her captor upon one of his frequent "inspections."

She had tried to escape a few times. She kicked and screamed for a couple days, then tried to run a couple times. But the doors were always locked and as the beatings and sexual punishments worsened with each attempt, her foul-breathed pimp had threatened her with death. "Run again, you little slut, and next time I'll kill you." She believed him and thoughtless compliance became her existence. And survival.

The routine became a sort of comfort, if it could be called that. The man with bad breath would enter, give her food and the drink of "control medicine," and then tell her (or force her) to lie down. "Lessons" continued daily until Amber no longer felt anything. Mechanically, she did as she was instructed and even the pain subsided. She felt no desire to leave. No care for what would happen. Her only desire was for the medicine, which brought the numbness and made her forget. Forgetting everything to exist in the moment, that was the real trick. But once a day, it was possible. And when a new man walked into her room with the medicine one day, she barely noticed.

Just to forget everything. That was all she wanted.

3

On the fourth day, the door handle rattled and one of her captors appeared, causing Amber to jump up.

"Hey. Get up. It's time for you to meet the other girls," barked a man Amber didn't recognize. She knew who he was didn't matter; obedience was her only requirement.

Bleary and disheveled, Amber stumbled out of the bed and followed him cautiously out of her room and to another locked door in the hallway. She'd passed this and the other doors going to the bathroom, which was always monitored and after which, she was locked back in her own room. The burly man unlocked the door and stepped into a large living room filled with at least a dozen girls talking and watching an old TV. The windows were covered with cardboard allowing only dim sunlight. The main light emanated from two dusty, fringed lamps sitting on equally dirty end tables on either side of one of the orange sofas where thin girls of various sizes sat. Two old coffee tables posed like stubby statues in front of them on threadbare brown carpet. A kitchenette was to the right and dishes filled the sink. It smelled of stale cigarettes and old Chinese food.

Embarrassed by her appearance, Amber tried to blend into the paneled wall.

"Listen up," the man snapped. "This is the new girl. Who wants to give her the highlights of the evening activities?" Laughing at his perceived wit, he motioned quickly to the back of the room, and said, "Okay. Make sure she feels welcomed!" Amber's eyes flittered across the room searching for anything to bring sense to the scene. One girl turned slightly to look at her, then turned back to her television show. The rest ignored her. Glancing around he added, "And get this place cleaned up by four o'clock. It's action time ladies, and we don't want to disappoint the customers." And then pausing, for effect added, "Or the boss." The light chatter continued. Spinning on his shoes, he walked briskly to a door adjacent to the kitchen, pulled out a key chain, and left, slamming the door and locking it behind him.

Where had all these girls come from? Why hadn't she known they were here? Were they all stolen like her?

Please, somebody tell me something, she begged in her mind.

Finally, a small blonde girl rose from the coffee table and approached.

"What's your name, new girl?" Her hair was the color of fresh straw, contrasting the dull atmosphere.

"Amber."

"No, your new name."

Amber stared, confused and maybe a bit mesmerized by the girl's magical blue eyes.

20

"Or haven't they given you one yet?" the girl smiled, showing off perfect cheekbones. "My name's Kena. I was the new girl two weeks ago."

She spoke as if chatting with an old friend and gave Amber a quick but strong hug.

Amber blinked, her thoughts flashing like lights at a railroad crossing. Unable to think, she started to cry and finally whispered, "Please. Where are we?"

Kena cocked her head and ran her eyes over Amber. "Well, this won't do. Hungry?"

"Yeah." Amber wiped her eyes and crossed her bare arms over her growling stomach.

"Follow me. I make an awesome omelet!" Grabbing her hand, Kena led her to the kitchen, shooting out introductions as they passed the table. "That's Gena, Heidi, Ginger and Jaylene. Say hi."

"Hi," the girls all said and Amber held up a timid hand. "Hi."

Kena pulled eggs and butter out of the refrigerator and the other girls scattered like cockroaches to the living room.

"Sit down, Amber."

A rickety looking wooden chair laced with dried food and littered with crumbs sat nearby. She eased into it.

Turning swiftly to the cupboard, Kena rattled the pots and pans. "So. Tell me all about Miss Amber. Where you from? What happened? And how are you feeling? Any pain? I got remedies!"

Amber held her silence. But Kena persisted. "I want to be your friend."

"You don't even know me," Amber replied with as much sass as she could summon.

Kena smiled and laid her hand on Amber's arm. "Oh Amber, I know you." She chuckled. "I know you, so well."

She let Amber have her silence, cooking eggs and humming something to herself. The "omelet" was delicious, and from that day on, Amber had a friend.

Bound to this new crazy existence, Amber's brightest moments soon became her daily chats with Kena. The other girls often called her "crazy," and "mental Barbie," but Kena seemed to genuinely believe they just misunderstood her intentions so in turn she disregarded them.

"Who cares?" she said, winking. "I've got friends. And that's all that matters."

She had an opinion on everything and wasn't afraid to waste it on anyone. From food to music, to clothes and even religion, she could wax eloquent on any topic. Even if her audience was only herself, she loved to hear herself speak, and it seemed spiritual talk was her favorite.

"I'm a spiritual being" was one of her most-used phrases. "But I'm a Universalist."

"What's a universe-salis?" Amber asked.

"Universalist. It means I am one with the universe. I embrace all religions and ways of spirituality. What do you believe in Amber?"

"Right this moment? Nothing."

Kena considered. "I see. Like God doesn't care or this wouldn't have happened?" She didn't pause for Amber's approval. "Well. I think you are wrong there. It's all good. I accept my life."

Gathering her courage, Amber pressed for clarification. "What do you mean you embrace all religions? How is that even possible?"

"Easy. One day I say Hail Marys. The next I might pray to Allah, or Buddha. I like Buddha. He's a cute little chubby dude." She threw her head back and laughed hard and loud.

"Shut up, you little slut!" screamed a girl lying nearby on a turquoise leather couch.

Kena smiled and perfectly broke two eggs on the edge of the mixing bowl and dropped them in. "And I'm multi-talented," she added. Leaning close so as not to be heard, she whispered. "Screw them," she motioned at the living room, "Just a bunch of no imaginations. Not like you and me," she winked.

In the days that followed, Amber learned Kena was not exaggerating about her spiritual claims. Every time they talked it was a new mystical journey into the strange and bizarre world of Kena. Voodoo chants, pot smoking, ecstasy, and detailed introductions to new and fanciful notions completely foreign to Amber's sheltered mind. Today it was staring into prisms while smoking pot and calling it "new age." And after that, she told her about "animal spirits."

"Can you guess what mine is, Plains-Keeper?" Kena asked, using one of her many endearing nicknames for Amber. She twirled her blonde hair. "Giraffe. What do you think?"

Amber quipped, "Well, it's better than a lizard—or a spider!" They laughed so loud the curses and empty soda cans rained down like confetti.

The routine seldom varied, the girls were released from their individual rooms each day around two o'clock for supper and then allowed free time. Television, alcohol, marijuana, and other assorted drugs were readily available and permitted. But there were limits, "We can't have you so wasted, you can't perform for our guests," instructed her bosses. The girls were never allowed to call it sex. It was performance, like running an acting business. "Make the customer happy," was the golden rule and what went unspoken was "or you will be denied your personal pleasures and feel the backhand of the boss." Still, the afternoon window was Amber's favorite time and they both had one strict rule they agreed to. They never talked about what happened at night.

One afternoon, Kena strode into the room and said.

23

"Today, I'm an atheist."

"I thought you were trying out all religions," said Ginger, a three year veteran of the house.

"I am," Kena said.

"That's makes no sense, you fool," Ginger shouted. "Atheism means no religion, dumb butt," she said, shaking her head.

"Actually, having no religion is a religion," Kena shot back. Kena had said Ginger was nothing more than a "sad, little bully." But she was also scared of her as she had a mean temper, and loved to smack the girls around.

"She hits you in the back and the legs, so the bruises aren't noticeable," Kena had cautioned. "Be careful."

Ginger snorted her disgust, while Amber smiled at her friend's complete disregard. It was one of the many things she loved about Kena. Her ability to maneuver through landmines and emerge completely unscathed. It blew her mind, honestly. And it wasn't just the pot Kena constantly encouraged her to smoke.

"What about Jesus," Amber asked one afternoon while they drank vodka and Sprite while nursing a joint.

"Oh, I know Jesus. He's cool. And, he's really kind of hot with that long hair and beard, don't you think?"

Amber laid her head back on the couch and laughed. "Yes. Now that I think about it. He is kind of hot!"

They both laughed. It was the best time she could remember having. Just to forget. Just to know someone cared for something besides what she could give them, besides using her body. As the days ground out, Amber from Gilroy was melting away. Laying her head back on the couch, she closed her eyes and followed random thoughts through her foggy brain. Her mother once told her that if you do something enough, it'll become a habit. Struck by the notion, Amber concluded she was bound by a few new habits.

I think I like Mary Jane and Smirnoff way too much.

Oh, but she missed her parents and her old life. And when she was high or stoned she suddenly didn't miss her mom and dad so much.

Then suddenly, like the last rays of the sun before it set, the moment was gone and the sharp sting of reality smacked her in the face.

"Fifteen to show time, girls!"

No prince was coming to save her. Daddy would be so ashamed of what she'd become. "Yep," she paused. "Not gonna happen."

"What's not gonna happen?" Kena asked, flopping onto the couch beside Amber. "You . . ." Amber straightened and looked at her. ". . . getting this bottle of vodka!" She grabbed it and tilted her head back for a long, hard hit.

Laughing, she handed the bottle to Kena. "Time to drink!"

4

Searing her mind, like a sizzling pan dropped hissing into the sink, memories assaulted her and Amber remembered. Oh, how she remembered. The images flashed like snapshots taken only yesterday and she was back there, stuck in that hot, hard trunk of the car that carried her from the barn outside Gilroy to the concrete slab of South Chicago. Somehow she was there in the trunk with the headache again but also here facing the abandoned storefront. Her mind had separated from time and she was stuck in the doorway of both places.

Her hands bound, her mouth taped shut, Amber was dragged violently from the trunk by rough hands. Feeling began flowing again to her twisted extremities and needle-like pain pressed into her hands, legs and feet.

"You scream and I'll slap the crap outta you," snarled the man who had chased Amber down the road. "I mean it."

Amber surmised she was at a truck stop somewhere north of Kansas. The air was cooler than Kansas and the diesel fumes and sounds and light were swallowed in the darkness. Having grown up on a farm, she knew the smell of diesel. Soon, her eyes began adjusting to the blackness. Meghan stood beside her and two more unknown men marched toward them from the shadows. A transaction of grunted words and dollars, and then the new men came toward them.

Amber yelled and tried slipping her zip-tied hands around Meghan but one pulled her away as the other grabbed Meghan and held a rag to her face. Meghan's scream was cut short and Amber began sobbing uncontrollably.

"You come with me," the first man with sweaty palms groped at Amber.

"Get them outta here now," sweaty palms fired back.

"No!" screamed Meghan through the rag. "NO!!" She had fought bravely until passing out.

"Don't take me away from Amber. Please. Please! Don't leave me, Amber."

"Shut up!" the man holding the rag to her face had growled and the scene branded itself into Amber's senses as he wrenched Meghan toward a gray van.

"Let's go," the other one said to her.

Amber watched in disbelief as Meghan was dragged away, still sobbing. As the dawn's early rays cascaded across the horizon, their eyes locked. Meghan's last words formed on her lips like glass cracking under the weight of a heavy stone.

"Find me."

Amber gasped. Nodded. "I promise," she said. She had fought bravely until passing out.

She never saw Meghan again. Standing in the shop's front stoop, a tear slipped down Amber's cold face. Well, maybe she hadn't forgotten everything.

Like an endless repeating refrain, the years clicked relentlessly by. Her teenage years had vanished, and when she turned eighteen her stint in the "house" was over and she was transferred once again. His name was Big George Stevens and he mysteriously appeared to take control of his new "property." Like something sold in the stockyard, Amber was bought once again and without a second glance, her captors let her go.

At the time, she'd thought only of leaving Kena.

Another memory came unbidden with a shooting pain through her chest. She remembered Kena, and a familiar lump rose in her throat. Squinting her eyes shut so as to hold in the tears, she remembered.

Why were all her memories so painful?

"Pack your stuff," the one called Raul had bit at her, and without a word, Amber had marched to her room. She knew her time there was over, but she hadn't known what it meant. What would happen to her? And what would happen to her only friend?

Suddenly she felt a man's huge hands around her waist and turning her body gently, Big George's chubby fingers squeezed her face as he murmured.

"Come with me, baby. Big George will take good care of you. I'll give you everything you've ever wanted."

"I can't leave Kena," was all she'd said.

He'd shown her his perfect white teeth. "Then she can come too."

Reassured Kena would be coming later, Amber had followed George down the stairs and out the door like a trained monkey.

What else could she do? She had no money, no place to stay, no phone. Just the clothes on her back and the food in her stomach.

As long as she could stay with Kena, her life was anyone's for the taking.

5

She walked along the wide empty sidewalk, frozen.

She should never have left Kena.

Like so many of the girls, Kena was eventually sold to Big George and pushed onto the streets to become a walker. And despite his promise, Big George had denied Amber further communication with her which had scarred Amber more deeply than even losing Meghan.

Then, one day Amber heard the news that Kena had been found dead, and Amber's heart had broken beyond repair. Details were sketchy and most questions would remain forever sealed in a forgotten police file. There was something about a crazy John and a forty-eight hour binger with lots of drinking and drugs. Probably just Kena and her typical craziness.

But now she was dead. And the world could never be right again.

For weeks after, Amber had spiraled deeper and deeper into drugs and dissociative behavior. The deeper she went, the more she punished her body. Anything to forget the loss of her best friend, the loss of all she'd wanted or hoped for within this dark, lonely existence.

A girl with short red hair was approaching. "Hi. I'm Rachel. Can I ask you a question?" Without waiting for Amber's reply, Rachel dived in.

"Can you give me one reason why you stay on the streets?"

Amber hadn't been paying attention; otherwise, she'd have avoided this interaction. "You a walker?" Amber asked. Rachel was out awfully late. Giving her a quick glance, Amber let a small giggle escape. "Who are you?"

"Used to be a walker, just like you. Now I walk the streets talking to prostitutes."

Amber scoffed and shuffled on. "Well, no thanks."

"Just a second."

Bored, and slightly buzzed, Amber turned and looked at her. Rachel was slightly amusing in her "I [heart] Sex Workers" t-shirt. Amber waited, giving her the street language, "permission to engage."

"He changed my life," Rachel said.

"What was his name? I should give him a call." Amber chuckled.

"His name is Jesus."

"Oh," Amber's voice trailed and she turned to go. "I'm not talking about religion."

"That's fine. But think about my question? And here's my number. If you need anything, give me a call."

Amber nodded imperceptibly and continued on, losing the thread in the foggy jumble of words. But the question followed.

"Why do you stay?"

Why not hop on a bus and go home?

She scoffed. *Right. If only it was that easy.*

Still, the words would haunt her for days. First, if she was being honest, she was an addict. From the beginning, she'd learned to escape by detaching herself emotionally and mentally. She wasn't here most of the time anyway. She'd separated from her body but everyone else thought that was her. The *truth?* And it was impossible to deny. It stared back at her in the mirror: she was a prostitute. After six years and thousands of sexual encounters where she'd separated from her body, she could never be normal again. She'd never be anything else but a slut. "And if I went back now, everyone would know it." And the fact was, she was good at it. She'd been forced into it, true, but it had revealed her strength and true skill. She'd found her talent early and learned to control her tricks with subtle yet effective games. And all her clients knew it: she did it *well.*

I enjoy it. I do. How would they feel about that? *And the money is good.* I'm finally getting my due. No way I could make this much back at Gilroy.

A light rain began to fall mixing with her still damp cheeks. She had to get somewhere warm. Her teeth chattered and she pulled at her thin jacket as she headed toward home.

Home.

"Rest in peace, Kena. May all your pain be erased. I love you."

———

Amber woke with a gasp and fumbled for the lamp. The bulb popped as she turned it on and the brief flash of light only served to deepen the dingy gray of the morning through the thick curtains. It seemed blacker than usual. Despite the bright day outside, thick darkness spread through her cramped studio apartment and seemed to swallow everything. A blackness so deep it devoured even sound.

Amber lay motionless trying to breathe as she waited for her senses to adjust.

The idea that it was morning did nothing to soothe her anxious mind.

Though she'd tried to remain calm, a small terror crept into her body. It began behind her eyes and slowly grew and spread to her throat. Her breathing became shallower. Awake but half-asleep, she was back in the house of her captors and clamping her hand over her mouth, Amber stifled the scream threatening to leap from her lips.

Deprived of her senses, she perceived a shadow moving silently through the door and against the wall at the foot of her bed. She imagined gnarled fingers sliding around her neck and beginning to squeeze. Her breath stopped. Her mouth went dry and she choked. In a moment, she was subdued and helpless.

Like a silent fog, the malicious presence fed off the panic overcoming her, increasing in strength and dragging her deeper. A sour, bitter taste took over all senses. Kicking and thrashing, Amber fought the urge to vomit.

Unseen yet completely real, she fought the despair. She could not scream, could not run. What could she do? Where would she go? She was a girl destroyed, "damaged goods." A trashy prostitute. Again the squall of fear rose to choke her and smother her face.

"*Shhh . . .*" the presence hissed, as ghostly fingers stretched up to wipe her tears away.

Was this real?

I must not fight this or I'll die, she thought. Emptiness had always lived in the shadows, but now it sought to control her, to comfort her. To be her light.

She'd escaped the evil men who'd imprisoned her, but could she ever be truly free?

No. Escape was not possible. Only a fool would try. And to survive, was there any alternative but to stop fighting and give up? If she accepted this offer of comfort, wherever it was from, her hope would die but maybe she would live? Maybe without hope, it wouldn't hurt so much.

She was tired of the pain. And there was nothing left in her to offer a fight.

She laid back down, knowing she would not be sleeping anymore that morning.

———

Amber pounded at the alarm clock. It was 1:30 pm on a Wednesday afternoon. She could no longer sleep. It was warmer, but her body shivered beneath the splayed covers, she replayed in her mind the dream that daily reoccurred. Dreams had always fascinated her, but this one seemed to live between the place of waking and sleep. Hallucinations. Seeing what you expect to see. Soon your eyes start playing tricks on you. Only this time it isn't a trick. Without cause, fantasy becomes fictionalized truth. In the end, she thought, we're all defenseless to escape our dreams. Unable to flee, we are forced to re-live our past, our present or our future in a never-ending cycle of mindless repetition. Without deeper understanding, we become hostages to our nightmares. Stumbling through the day, our wits scattered like lint under the bed, writhing with blunted pain we walk squarely into our living daymare. *There is no escape.*

Helpless to control, hopeless to understand, hopeless to do anything, the freakish dream becomes reality.

Twenty years old and "Misty" was now a walker. Released from her six by ten room, she'd exchanged one prison cell for another but was now free to "walk"—though there was no freedom on the streets.

A walking tomb, she thought to herself. Her only task was to drum up clientele by walking the 14th and 15th block of West Street.

"You're still a looker," Big George had whispered in her ear earlier that afternoon. "But too old for the upstairs business. The boys on the street want a woman. Give them what they want and we'll give you what you need."

Amber felt her body twitch. Her bones began to tingle. She had heard the tales from the older girls and she had lived the risks vicariously through Kena and it scared her. Scared her deep in the marrow. She'd made a desperate plea.

"Please, Big George, don't make me go out there!"

Boom! Sparks of pain contracted her vision as Big George's mammoth hand flashed across and struck her head. Looming over her, his hulking body filled her room. "I hit you high so as not to leave a mark. But don't you ever, *ever* defy Big George. Do what I say. Any questions?"

"Sorry, Big George," she whimpered, straining to discern the rules to the new game. Raising her hands, she rubbed his legs. "No questions. I'm sorry."

"Good baby. That's good. Now get hustling."

It was her first night on the street, the one that would repeat in her head night after night like a song stuck on auto-play. The other girls on West street looked at her like she was a psycho just let loose from the asylum. Muttering and crying, she was a sad sight on the streets of south Chicago that night.

"So this is my reward, God? " she yelled to a smog-filled night sky. "Really? Six years of service and now I get promoted. Flipping cool, I say. Flipping cool. Aren't I lucky?" she screeched at the bum sleeping on the steps of a closed office door. "So blessed! Yeah. That's it. Blessed."

Then like a kaleidoscope swirling through images, her mood morphed into something ugly and morbid. Self-pity reached new depths and she screamed.

She crumpled to the sidewalk and slowly looked up. No one seemed to notice.

"Now that I think about it," she said to herself, "I probably do deserve this. I know God that you remember. Oh yeah. You know. You remember don't you?

Turning her back away from the street, she pulled tight her jacket, stared into the empty window of a bookstore and thought, *For all the crap I've said and done.*

Glancing into the window, her reflection cast a distorted shadow and she paused, mesmerized by its strangeness. "You saw me do those things, and now I get my just desserts. When I started cursing. And when I let Mark Ryder touch me. And when I stole that money from Dad's wallet. And that beer at Meghan's party. That's why, huh? This is what I get, right, this life?"

She murmured to the reflection. "I get it. I'm a bad person. I deserve this. I really do."

The sound of a fist smacking a palm echoed across the deserted street like a beast attacking its prey. Big George moved into the reflection and suddenly, her reverie was broken.

Immediately she understood, and like a good little soldier, Amber turned and marched back into the field of battle. Unzipping her jacket and pulling the neckline of her blouse down, she saddled up to the black Lexus that glided up beside her.

"Hey baby!" she crooned. "Wanna have some fun?"

The man was in shadow, but she climbed into the car anyway. She glanced once more into the darkness behind her and whispered, "My name is Misty. I'm a walker."

She was out of the cold icy wind and for a moment, it allowed her to escape her present reality. The man was silent next to her and she watched the city pass, remembering that summer vacation to the "windy city" so long ago. A watery tear slid down her cheek, warming her face. The memory crashed into her mind.

"Why is it called the windy city?" Amber had asked as they passed Wrigley Park where they watched the Chicago Cubs play. They were on their way with her older siblings Eric and Grace to Shedd Aquarium to see all the brightly colored fishes. And after that had come pizza. Wonderful thick Chicago pizza. In a moment, she remembered it all.

"Daddy," she whispered, "Where are you?"

Within an hour, she'd stumble back onto the sidewalk and continue her aimless drift.

6.

"Life is a mysterious thing. It snatches up our loved ones and swallows them whole. Suddenly without warning, the opportunity to say goodbye is gone."

He had read it in a book, and at first he dismissed it as the musings of a slightly demented mad man. After, all how could anyone believe a fourteen year-old girl could be snatched right from under her parents' noses? Or that God would even allow it? Yes, there were the occasional stories and even horrific accidents, but an abduction? Just gone? Vanished without a trace?

So for the hundredth time, Ray dug through the dusty, disorganized piles of books on his shelves and finally found the words for which he sought.

"Life will not wait or explain itself. We must take the time we have and make whatever amends we can while we still have breath."

Only after he'd lost his little girl did the desperate words make sense. Maybe he was the demented mad man now.

The disappearance of Amber and Meghan had shocked the little town, the surrounding community, and left Ray, his wife Amanda, and his two other children perpetually numb and lifeless. Ray truly loved them all, but Amber was his baby. And she was a beautiful child. There was a spirit about her that was contagious. Friendly and outgoing, with long black hair and bright green eyes, she was loved by all.

For four years, he'd searched. And Ray became undone.

Everyone in Gilroy seemed desperate to compartmentalize the abduction and call it something else—a "tragedy," a "horrible event"—as if affixing a label and eliminating all the terrible confusion and pain into a single word could erase the unspeakable reality and undo the evil.

But there was no containing the horror. And in four grueling years, they'd found no suspect, no closure, no explanation. No Amber.

The statewide search had been long and exhaustive. Thousands of man-hours were expended. And Ray, unable to sit idly by while his daughter was likely suffering, began daily driving hundreds of miles on deserted country roads searching for any clue, any sign of his precious youngest daughter.

Returning nightly to the old farmhouse, his truck was caked with dirt and mud accumulated from countless dead ends. And now he'd spent several more fruitless days searching.

Ray stumbled into the kitchen, dumped his duffel on the floor and slowly lowered his beaten frame into the wooden spooled chair. He didn't hear Amanda come in from the living room and set her book down on the table.

"Where have you been?"

Jolted from his stupor, Ray jumped to his feet and reached for her. "Amanda, I'm sorry . . ."

"Don't touch me! You do not get to apologize and make everything okay. I am sick of it. Sick of it all." Pausing only to suck in a breath, she hugged herself as if afraid of flying apart. And maybe she was.

"I call the store and you aren't there. But where? I'm here. Here Ray. Every day. Taking care of the kids, driving them around, talking to the detectives. Cooking, cleaning."

Ray knew better than to say anything until she was done. Soon, she was crying and pounding her fists on his chest. Ray waited helplessly as the sobs poured from his wife. Grabbing her hands, he held her close with his other arm but suddenly she pulled back and something flashed in her eyes. Determination or a new decision, he couldn't tell which, and then she raced for the bedroom. Hearing the lock click, he prepped for another sleepless night on the pullout sofa.

Little did he know that would be the last time he held her in his arms.

What else could he do? He knew she'd descended into a fog of sleeping pills, old movies and magazines. The kids were often pawned off like hand-me-down clothes to the relatives. The house was a mess. Piles of junk littered the floors, dirty dishes crammed the sink, and the stink of soiled laundry and unwashed toilets gave the air a stockyard quality. Like an island breaking off of the shore, a chasm had built between them that slowly turned love and devotion into a daily drift of apathy and agony.

Ray stepped out of the screen door, over a collapsed tower of books, and over to the porch swing. Spider webs attached it to the railing and floor. Foggy particles and drops of water hung in the fall air. The days and months had unfolded, the hunt for Amber and Meghan had become more desperate, and then more hopeless. Local investigators had been forced to turn the case over to the FBI once they suspected the girls had been taken across the state line. After sixty days, the search had come to an end.

What day was it? Sometime in October, Ray thought. The cold crept into Ray's bones and moved to his heart and lodged in his spirit. Like a tumor burrowing into the membranes of a healthy organ, it ate away at Ray, devouring him piece by piece, bite by bite.

He recalled his last moments with the agents. Their feeble attempts to comfort a broken, despondent father and mother burned across his mind.

"Why can't anyone tell me what happened?" he'd asked. "How no one saw this guy or knows where he took them is beyond my understanding."

One by one, Ray's penetrating stare had caused each of them to dip their chins and kick silently at the dead grass in Ray's front yard. "One day they were here and the next they were gone? I don't care if you're done looking, it's my job to find my daughter."

He'd given up and quietly moved to his pickup truck. The only sound in the fading light had come from Amanda crying on the porch. The old door had groaned as Ray climbed in. "I know you can't hear her. But I can. Every day. She's out there asking, 'Where's my daddy? When's he coming to get me?'"

Cranking the starter, he'd shoved the transmission into drive and slipped down the gravel road that eased onto Kansas highway 37. Light was draining from the sky, shortening the horizon, and making it unfamiliar. But Ray had already lost his way.

Children had disappeared for reasons unknown. Reasons that were disappearing into the long Kansas landscape. Ray had driven for hours down forgotten hunting lanes, peering into abandoned buildings and past dormant fields of rotting cornstalks. Finally, pounding his fists on the dashboard, he'd helplessly turned the wheel and begun the journey back home, though now he knew it only as the place where he lived. He'd realized he could no longer call it home, its empty rooms and forgotten memories. Just a fragmented collection of reminders of a former life, eclipsed by the sucking darkness in his heart and mind.

He blinked back the memory and looked out over the fields. The kids were away at his parents' again, but the cries from Amanda in their bedroom sounded like his daughter's. It was exactly how she'd sounded the night they realized the search was over. The glow had been visible for miles down the wide-open horizon of the Kansas plains. At first he'd panicked, wondering if the farm was on fire. But turning down the lane leading to the house, he saw the cause. The illumination drew him long before he understood its meaning. Hundreds of people lined the gravel driveway holding candles that flickered like a long line of fireflies through the summer night. Friends, family and strangers stood in silent vigil as he passed in his truck. The show of solidarity and support broke across Ray like a wave crashing across the bow of a ship, and his eyes glazed with a strange mix of gratitude and resentment. Some held signs, others held flowers, many wept, but each stood still in remembrance of his beloved Amber.

When he'd finally made it to the front drive, he'd turned off the truck and let huge sobs of sorrow rack his body. The reality of the day had burst upon him like a flash flood whipping down a gully and it was then he'd realized the candle vigil wasn't just a show of community support, it was a deathwatch. They were declaring the end of the journey, accepting that Amber was lost. Probably dead. And they all knew it.

He'd sat there, paralyzed with a frustration so deep it scared him. There would never be answers. Only unspoken questions heaped atop the unsolved riddle of the disappearance of two children.

What could we have done? Who would do this? And why?

Of all the questions, that one, that hellacious *why* pierced him like a javelin and clung like a giant leech sucking the life from his bones.

Who could he hold responsible?

The questions had been consuming him for more turns of the calendar than he could remember, much less admit. Too long he'd resisted the nagging in his gut over who was ultimately responsible. And that secret had fueled his tireless search. His bloodless resolve to rise each day and begin the search anew took root in that silence, the night he had made up his own answer.

His hands had quivered on the steering wheel. Amanda and the kids had been at his parents so they hadn't seen the vigil.

He'd barely made it inside before collapsing in the entry.

The door to her room hung slightly ajar, inviting Ray to push it open. A soft creak announced him to the trophies and stuffed animals on the shelves, exactly as she'd left everything over six years earlier. As he cautiously stepped into Amber's room, it felt startlingly empty, devoid of all humanity, though the sordid collection of evidence of a typical young girl's life bore witness to the loss of everything whole and good, all happiness they once held now dissipated.

The world quietly lay sleeping in their beds but for Ray, sleep was not an option. Only one thing consumed his mind.

Glancing around at the memories of Amber's life, the reality of his failure burst fresh into his heart. Sitting on the edge of her bed, he listened, the only sound, the magnified ticking of her alarm clock.

Tick. Tick. Tick.

He had found what he'd been looking for.

He'd kept the realization at bay for years, but the ticking off of lost moments and unlived memories was relentless.

The guilty party was no longer obscured. Justice would be served.

In the end, I know who I was looking for, thought Ray. *I've found the one responsible.*

He was a man who didn't pay attention, often said a cross word and cast a disapproving eye. He was a man who had done nothing but in doing that, did everything.

He'd found him. And he would be punished.

His wife, his family, and his daughter had all disappeared into a puff of Kansas dust and life as he knew it had left him.

He could stop searching. There was no use. No excuse. Life had spit in his face and shown him for who he really was: a failed father.

And nothing could alter the fact that he was the reason Amber had been stolen.

———

They never found Johnnie or her abductors. The disappearance remained an unsolved case. And as the years rolled by, no new clues emerged.

Those girls were dead and everyone knew it.

He'd learn to avoid the people who would offer condolences as he stumbled to work or the grocery store. *Such a terrible tragedy.*

Amanda would move on. She'd leave Gilroy, unable to sustain any semblance of a proper mother or woman. Beaten and destroyed, she'd take the kids and move three hours to the big city of Wichita where she could hide. And Ray would feel the sting of a broken marriage. He would again experience the loss of his children as the fractures continued to splinter their lives like a window shattering in slow-motion before his eyes.

Those who could help offered encouragement and occasional gifts and money. They cared, but what could anybody do?

He was thinking it was a Thursday as Ray slowly pushed his cart down the aisle of the grocery store. Through the discontented fog of his thoughts, Ray overheard the conversation.

"Heard they arrested a couple geezers over in Menlo for trafficking girls to Chicago."

Ray listened intently nodding and hurrying through his transaction until he caught up with one of the men exiting the store.

"Marc," Ray jogged up to him across the parking lot.

The man turned. "Hey, Ray. Haven't seen you around. How's it going?"

A local contractor, Marc Gooden was always friendly with Ray at the hardware store and had known Amber, though they'd never talked about the abduction specifically.

"Maybe. Listen," Ray said. "I overheard you mention an arrest for sex trafficking."

"Oh, man," Marc mumbled dropping his head. "Ray, I'm sorry."

"No." Ray held up his hand. "I'm just curious what else you might have heard."

"Not much really." Marc stood in front of his truck looking uncomfortable. "Just two scumbags selling girls to some outfit in Chicago. Hope they rot in jail."

Stepping into the conversation break, Ray quickly asked, "You think they might have been doing this a while?"

Marc hesitated. "Don't know. But I'd say," and he paused. "It's a good chance." Marc stuck out his hand. "It's good to see you, Ray."

"Hey, you too. I'm sorry, Marc. Hope I didn't bother you."

"Not at all. I'm the one who's sorry." Marc opened the door to his truck and climbed in and Ray started to walk to his truck.

"Hey Ray?" Marc shouted over the roar of the engine.

"Yeah?" Ray turned slowly.

Marc took a moment. "You thinking Amber's alive?"

Ray blinked back anger and answered slowly. "I do."

Marc nodded, then shook his head. "My prayers are with you, man. Godspeed."

"Thanks. I'll take' em."

Resuming his crawl toward his truck, Ray whispered to himself. "I'll take whatever prayers I can get."

7

It was 3:00 o'clock in the morning. Ray sat in his recliner with the legs kicked out, snugly tucked into the leather confines. It should have been comfort at its finest, only comfort was the elusive creature that had slipped away and left for good. Joy was a word he couldn't seem to place. Gravel rolled in his gut and sand slid down his throat. His eyes shut, his body immobilized, he awaited the restlessness of sleep, but behind his clenched eyelids, mortar shells of hopelessness erupted as he maneuvered a minefield of regret and blame.

Why was I so gruff with her but also so easy on her? Amanda was right. I worshiped her. I put her on a pedestal and now she's gone. I should have insisted—no—I should have demanded she stay from that piece of trash Johnny.

For a moment, Ray stopped babbling and imagined he saw Johnny's face. Suddenly, he was squeezing the life out of him, reality fleeing from his mind.

Why didn't I kill him while I had the chance? I should have made her stay in the store. I should have punished her for disobeying me.

Pushing the recliner back, Ray burrowed even deeper, his bed for the night. Not only was he an unfit father, he was an impotent man.

The thought seized him *I'm a faker.* A weak, pathetic excuse for a man. *If only I'd been a real father.*

His eyes filled with fluid and his nose bubbled. Ray gasped for breath and lowered the chair. Sliding forward, Ray hung his head on his palms and let the emotions come. Tears flowed onto the rug on the hardwood floor.

If only I had tried harder instead of always going off to work, ignoring my duty and running off to the workshop and taking everything for granted. If I hadn't cared more for the fields than I did my own family, maybe then I wouldn't have blood on my guilty hands—trying to stop my guts spilling out.

"It's like I gave her up on the field of battle," he said out loud, Only Poseidon the cat was there. And he wasn't listening. Ray whispered to himself. "And I was completely helpless to stop it."

He was slowly starving to death. The unstoppable emotions coursed through his cells threatening to overrun his body. Bewilderment. Rage. Fear. And at the bottom of it all, shame. Shame like an endless coiling serpent leading him through an overgrown canopy of choking uncertainty and despair.

It's all right in front of me. I can taste my bitter failure. Everything I ever dreamed of for myself, my family, for Amber is gone.

It became his routine. Every night, Ray felt the darkness creep in and experienced the panic again, the overwhelming fear and deep shame reaching out to pull him into the blackness.

How can this be my life? What happened to me? How do I stop loving my Amber-lamb?

You can not, Ray suddenly heard. *You never will.*

He fell forward onto his knees. "Oh, God, forgive me! Oh, Amber! Please forgive me!"

At that moment, nothing else mattered but that one thing: he had found a shred of hope. Where had it come from?

Love never gives up. Amber is out there.

Whether it was hope or insane wishful thinking, he knew that as long as he lay here in that chair, that house, he was trapped. He was so tired of feeling pathetic.

The quietness of the moment engulfed the space as Ray sat silent, listening. "God, show me what to do!"

A stillness settled over him, then slowly new thoughts began to pluck at the recesses of his brain. Coupled with a fresh consuming zeal to attempt this enormous task of going in search of her again, the conviction put into motion forces that propelled him to forget every protection he'd come to trust in and fall blindly off the precipice into the insanity of this strange new hope.

It was time to seek and save that which was lost.

Ray felt the buzz before he heard the jangle of his cell phone. Holding it in front of his bleary eyes he read the caller ID. Pastor Tommy. He'd been Ray's pastor at Gilroy Community for over 15 years. A solid man of faith, Tommy's heart was always for God's best for Ray.

Ray knew it. *But still,* he thought.

He started to silence it, but instead, against his will, he answered.

"Hi Pastor Tommy. Everything okay? It's 3:00 in the morning."

"Hey Ray? I was praying and your name kept coming to me. How's it going?"

"Well—"

"I couldn't sleep either," Tommy said. "Then something told me to call you."

He hadn't been to church in months. "I guess it was a sudden moment of clarity," Ray said. "Like when you know that you know what you have to do."

There was silence on the other end. Then finally, "Ray, sometimes we have to be broken down to realize we weren't meant to carry our burdens alone."

Ray nodded, then realized and said, "Yeah." Should he tell him? That he had to resume the search for Amber? "I appreciate you calling," Ray said.

"You're going after Amanda, aren't you?"

Ray gulped. "No," he whispered. "I'm going after Amber."

It really wasn't much of a decision in hindsight. He knew Tommy would understand. His wife and kids were gone, but he could get them back. He had to go after the lost sheep, the one who had vanished like a snowflake in the desert. "I still deeply love Amanda and I know she loves me. But this pain. It's settled between us like ice and it burns us every time we try to move on. We can't ignore it. And I finally know what I have to do."

"Well, apparently God thought you could use a little extra encouragement."

Ray nearly cried again. But he held it together while Tommy prayed and he thanked him and hung up, feeling tired and surprisingly eager to sleep for the first time in as far back as he could recall.

That night would stick in Ray's thoughts like the memory of the best meal, resurfacing again for a fresh taste. Hope had leveled him, brought him to his knees and stripped away the last shred of dignity and manliness.

He'd finally admitted he no longer cared about anything but finding Amber. Everything else would follow that.

———— .·

Ray woke with a start in the chair. He dug for his cell, saw it was nearly dead and plugged it in.

Pastor Tommy's call last night had been strange. And he'd assumed Ray was going after Amanda.

If only he knew how things had gone down. "I'm leaving," Amanda announced with such casualness it made Ray think she was joking.

"Are you serious?" he asked, a bit broken. He didn't want to believe it, but he knew she was dead serious.

"I'm done." Again only two words, as if any more would disrupt the fragile fibers of control barely holding back the grief and despair that seeped from every room of the house.

"What do you mean?"

"It's your fault." She had stated it flatly, so precise, so final that Ray couldn't escape the fact she believed it.

And just like that, his wife and children were gone.

Sure, he still had his shop, but he'd lost all interest in that too shortly after Amber's disappearance.

Like everything else, it would only return once he came back. With her.

There was nothing to stop him now but fear. And he'd already faced the worst kind. The thought fused in his mind, cast like red-hot metal in a new mold.

He must find Amber. Or die trying.

———— .·

The first glint of morning sun crept into Ray's chamber. Thin and shimmering, the light created a brilliant glow upon the wall.

SEPULCHRE

Illumination, tiny and fierce, it crackled through the air set to
ignite the damp atmosphere like tinder.

Ray rose, hoisting his body like a man reborn.

He began searching the internet for information on sex trafficking. The amount and specificity was overwhelming and made
him sick to his stomach. It was difficult to swallow for several
hours. Yet he persisted in gaining knowledge about the local sex
trade economy and Chicago's dark underbelly. He had to. If she
was alive, Amber's life depended on it. But it was more than that.
His wife's life, his marriage, and the secure lives of his children
depended on it.

A plan began to form in his mind. It was risky, yes, even dangerous. But he must endeavor. To do nothing was impossible. He
would make whatever effort was needed. And if need be, he would
move heaven and earth to find Amber and bring her back.

8

Amber pulled out her secret iPod, the one possession she guarded with her life. If one of the bosses or Big George knew she had it, they'd probably "teach her a lesson." Nothing that took the girls away from their one task in life was allowed.

Glancing at the clock she noted the time. Four am. Sighing, she searched for her favorite song. She found it and popped in her earbuds. The music and words soothed her and calmed her spirit.

Like most teenaged girls Amber had wanted the world. But in a flash, it had flown away and only in her dreams did she even remember such a thing as real life.

So true, she thought, listening to the song. In the day, in the morning, when she finally closed her eyes, she flew away and forgot the hurt, the loss and the shame. Her daydreams—those most people had at night—were her only escape. Her imagination was her ultimate destination. She closed her eyes and dreamed of paradise.

She knew that for most, dreams meant little to them. If people talked of their dreams, it was usually their nightmares or strange, meaningless things. But when your life is the nightmare, your dreams become your only escape, and often your one chance at a real life. Anyone who's lived through hell can tell you, a dream can become more real than your day-to-day life. A trapped mind can make a false experience feel truer than reality.

No matter what you label experience, "dream" or "reality," a memory is created, Amber mused. *So who's to say a memory doesn't matter because it didn't really happen. Is it not still 'real?'*

Sleep for Amber—what little of it she got—was punctuated by persistent dreams. And they maintained a strong hold on her.

This morning, the triadic cycle began with dreams of her father. Passing through like a shadow, she flew over her father's old shop. He lay on a wooden bench out front, moaning and clutching his stomach. Writhing in pain, he tossed his head from side to side. He uttered unintelligible words and she hovered closer to hear.

"Amber, my dear one. Where are you? I know you are scared. I'm so . . . I'm so . . ."

"Daddy!" she called.

Then he vanished.

"Daddy, I'm okay!" she called in the darkness, but soon she was gliding through the open second story window to her old bedroom and she saw her mother nestling into her white-trussed canopy bed. Its familiar ruffles, lined with stuffed animals and dollies, held her mother in the soft sheets. But there were tears in her eyes and she moaned as well.

"Oh, Amber, my love! Please come home . . ."

She tried to respond, but like a windstorm rushing down a dusty plain, Amber was suddenly ripped from her bedroom. Her stomach somersaulted and she found herself sitting alone in her secret place. A place unknown to anyone else, it became her personal sanctuary when she discovered it one day while walking in the forgotten back field of her uncle's farm. Unbeknownst to her, hollows in the earth could sometimes appear in the fields. Carved caves of grass and weeds, they were a nuisance to the farmer, but to a desperate teenager seeking solace, it was sanctuary. Here she'd often gone to shed tears of frustration. Here her heart was refueled. In this simple hollow, the monsters had abated, and Amber had found escape from the pressures of small town life.

As the youngest of three, she'd known precious few places of peace and solitude. Though she'd grown up attending church, it hadn't become her own faith as the weeks and years rolled by. But now, seared deep within her memories, the songs, the messages of hope and the kindness of that community returned to her.

Maybe she still remembered a little something.

"Something about . . . your word I have hid in my heart," she said aloud. "That I might not sin against you God." She laughed. "Well, I guess that didn't happen!"

Now, the memory of her secret place beckoned as her inner sanctum.

Here, surrounded by the tall grass in the field of the childhood preserved in her mind, she pulled out the thin black book and began to read.

> In the beginning the Word already existed. He was with God, and he was God. He was in the beginning with God. He created everything there is. Nothing exists that he didn't make. Life itself was in him, and this life gives life to everyone. The light shines through the darkness, and the darkness can never extinguish it.

Amber laid down the book. The verses swam like vibrant fish. She heard them, but they yielded no understanding.

He? The Word of God is a He? Why hadn't she realized that before?

Suddenly, on the edge of her vision, a movement caught her eye and she scanned the thick tufts of seedy alfalfa. Fear crept up on her and slowly rose, but Amber ignored it and looked closer. She was a field mouse entranced by the beady eyes of a rattlesnake. Her gaze sharpened and soon, a wavy form appeared and she could hear rustling as the apparition approached. She realized it was a man walking toward her.

A farmer's cap on his head and a stalk of grass hung from the corner of his mouth. Brown hair protruded from beneath the hat and his cheeks glistened beneath his full brow. His checked shirt with sleeves rolled up and faded jeans over boots made her think it was her farmer uncle strolling through his fields.

Had he seen her or was there still a chance she might escape notice?

Uneasiness nipped at her and she crouched into the hollow. He raised his hand and gave a slight wave. Amber weakly waved back.

Her senses leaped to flight when she saw it was not her uncle but a younger man, one vaguely familiar who was now stepping into her personal space. She felt the fear slip away and a strange warmth seeped into her, through her muscles and into her spirit. His presence seemed to give her power and made her rise to throw off the fear that held her captive.

"Amber," he said and the warmth grew.

"Jesus?" This was a dream, right? Maybe she could decide what happened.

He smiled and stuck out his hand. She silently reached for it and in a moment, she thought she could imagine being whole again. Healthy. Home.

"Jesus," she said again, feeling lost in the deep stillness of his kind eyes.

When her hand touched Jesus, nothing prepared her for the jolt, the rush of wind, her universe unfolding like a kaleidoscopic flower. Ribbons of color flew from his face and hands and images suggesting hidden knowledge fanned out and suddenly she was aware of an immensity within and beyond her, of limitless *life* pulsing all around her.

Light in patterns and swirls of color she'd never dreamed of. Light defying any logic and reason. Light shining through every darkness. Light beyond belief but demanding it, demanding a response. A response to this man.

"I think we know each other, Amber," he said.

"I remember you," she said still holding his hand.

"We used to talk all the time," he paused and looked around. "Right here, in fact."

Like a torrent rushing from a fresh downpour, relief flowed into Amber's veins and words poured from her mouth. "Jesus, where have you been? Why have you left me here in this place? Where's my dad and why hasn't he come for me? My heart is breaking, Jesus. It's broken. It bled out long ago. Now I'm nothing more than a used-up piece of rotting trash." She choked and sobbed, trying to catch her breath.

"No, Amber. You are my precious child. And I am here now," he gently said.

Amber gulped air and felt his hand around her neck, his head suddenly holding hers up. "But why? Why did you take so long? I thought you loved me! I don't understand. Please. Can I go home with you?"

"Oh, sweet girl. Listen, you *are* home with me. Here, and always."

She wanted to believe it, but—she stood up. "Then why don't I feel you with me always? Why do I feel so far from you, so dirty and ashamed?" She focused on breathing. "Do I need to be forgiven?"

"Amber, I already forgave you long ago. I've always been here but you see me now because you cried out. I am close to the broken, the contrite in heart. I see all of you, and I love you."

Blinking back her tears, the truth and comfort of his words crashed into her heart and somehow knit her back together.

He placed a hand on her shoulder. "Contrary to popular belief, I don't hide from people. I seek you out. I came for you and I only ask you to receive me now as who I am, as God's only son."

She sniffed and nodded.

"The problem is not a lack of access to God," he continued. "That was taken care of long ago. The problem is blaming God the Father for the evil in this life. It is lack of faith and belief in God's love that keeps you from seeing me and accepting the life I came to bring."

"So you're like a figment of my—?" she'd only begun to whisper it, but couldn't finish the thought. She didn't want him to be just a dream. "How do I know you are really Jesus? Please tell me this isn't just in my head. I need to know the truth."

"Who do you say I am?" Jesus asked. "That's all that matters. Can I tell you a story I heard?"

Amber sat back down. "Sure."

Jesus sat nearby and leaned back on his elbows in the grass. "A great king fell in love with a poor, humble servant girl. He could have any woman in the kingdom, yet he loved the servant girl, so he pondered how to win her love. Would she love him or fear him? Would she say she loved him only because he was the king? Would she come to miss her old life and loathe him? How could he ever know if she truly loved him while he was still king?

There was only one way he surmised he could make the unequal match equal. He must accept her life, her world. So he clothed himself in servant's clothes and yielding all his power, he renounced his throne. You see, he sought not first her respect or honor, but her love and her commitment in marriage."

"Oh, I like him!" said Amber. "And I think I get it. You did all that. You're the king." She looked up and met his eyes. "And if you love me like that, then how can I not believe in you?"

"Good, Amber. That is a great start." Jesus smiled and the warmth once again seeped into Amber's frame. Part of the darkness slipped from her and out into the simmering shadows creeping across the sky.

Suddenly, Jesus stood and stretched. "Remember. My light shines in the darkness, and the darkness can not overcome it."

"Jesus?" Amber watched him turn and head back the way he'd come. The last rays of sunlight dropped from the horizon and across the burnt orange sky. Momentarily blinded, Amber shielded her eyes, and as her vision returned, she realized he was gone.

9

Amber woke to a darkening sky. Reality stepped in front of the last images of her reverie and reminded her it was almost time for work.

The horrible sinking feeling returned. It had been only a dream, just as she'd suspected.

She willed herself up to sit on the edge of the wrinkled bed. If she was honest, there were times she wanted to end it all. Find a gun. Stick it in her mouth and blow her head off. Hell didn't seem all that frightening. At least she would be free. But it was a miracle that she had found the little black book. And there was no denying that a new hope, a different sort of life support was creeping into her.

Everything within her wanted to turn and run back to the field to be with Jesus. Why had he said he was always with her? If that was true, where had he gone?

She got dressed and went out for a quick bite, then work, back and forth from street to apartment and nodding at the other girls and her boss a few times, until dawn broke and the last john left. Another horrendous day had finally concluded.

Her head buzzing, tongue laced with thickness, she stumbled into bed and fell face first into her sheets.

Disgusted, she stripped the bed, her apparatus of torment and escape, and hurled the thin linen into the corner of her prison. This whited sepulchre of death would not claim her any longer. She had to find a way out.

She collapsed on the naked bed and watched the faint electronic light from her digital alarm clock cast a blue glow on her wall. She focused on the pattern, the luminous color changing as she rolled her eyes from side to side. The light soothed her mind and the emptiness of her night began to fall away.

She was escaping. Silently her eyes closed.

———

Out of the darkness, a man's image materialized with the grassy landscape.

Jesus was there.

She ran to her safe place, and dispensing with customary greetings, Amber gritted her teeth. "Tell me what it means, Jesus."

"Tell you what, Amber?" His seed hat was slightly askew and his tone and demeanor immediately soothed her like cool aloe on sun-baked skin. He seemed to ease the burn of pain from Amber's mind and spirit.

"Help me to understand what it means to be made new. That's what I want so badly. How can I ever be clean again after all that has happened?" She paused to catch her breath, the words hanging desperate like a sudden thundercloud preparing to release its heavy burden. "I remember a sermon Pastor Tommy preached about Nicodemus, the man who wanted to know how to be born again after he was old.'"

Jesus smiled. "I remember that service. I sat right beside you that day. You were listening."

"I didn't always," Amber said quietly.

"No one does," Jesus said. "I often ignored things religious leaders were saying so I could hear God's voice better." He adjusted his cap and leaned back into the grass like before. "And by the way, thank you for asking. For seeking the truth. I love that about you."

"I guess I knew that," Amber said, almost to herself. "But it's nice to hear."

"You see, Amber, everyone who's born once must be born again. The pious and prayerful and even teachers of Scripture. No one can see God's kingdom unless they are born again."

"But why?" Amber tilted her head.

"I know you can understand this," Jesus said. "When you want to share spiritual truth and no words will express it, you have two options. You can try new words, which nobody will understand, or you can use old words in a new way. I chose the 'old-word' method"

"Like making the words reborn," Amber said out loud.

Jesus grinned wide. "Exactly. Words like light, wind, water and bread, you give them new meaning when you relate them to spiritual concepts. The bread of life. The wind of the spirit. That kind of thing."

Amber picked a stalk of grass and flattened it between her fingers. "I get it. So you did the same thing with the idea of being born."

"So now you need to know how you can be reborn," Jesus said, looking deep into her face.

Amber nodded emphatically. "But I can't go back and change what's happened."

Jesus leaned forward. "Physical birth brings physical nature. When you experience spiritual birth, you have God's nature. Change your mind about your spiritual condition and you change who you are. Remember what John the Baptist said?"

"What," Amber wiped her eyes with her sleeve. She saw it was white and wondered where it had come from.

"He said, 'Repent.' That's what it means to be reborn." Jesus laid a hand on Amber's arm.

Amber looked down and shook her head slowly from side to side.

"My father loved the world so much that he ensured everyone who believed in me could live forever. I know you feel helpless, lost and trapped by evil. But there's a loving Father for a sinning world, and anyone can have certain salvation who's willing to accept me as their Savior. Nicodemus needed to realize his utter helplessness. That's all. He got that. And eventually, he realized that's what made salvation possible. It's only by faith in me, the Son of God."

"I know you feel dirty, unworthy and ashamed."

Once again Amber let tears slip from her eyes.

Jesus reached for her chin and lifted her head. "What do we do with that?"

"I don't know," she sobbed. "I feel so worthless. Call it what it is. I'm a . . . a prostitute."

"Oh, Amber, " Jesus moaned. "No."

"You don't need to ask forgiveness for that. You haven't been given many options. But please. Please." Jesus's words trailed off and the next words spoken to Amber were charged with emotion. "You are forgiven. God did not send me to condemn you, but to save you. When you believe, you are not condemned."

"I want that, Jesus. I really do," Amber sighed. "But why do you even want to help me?"

"I've been abducted, abandoned and forsaken, and I've done terrible things in response . . . I even blamed God."

"And me?" Jesus completed her sentence.

"Yes." Amber weakly replied her head dropping.

"But you want to be reborn, " Jesus lovingly responded. "Don't be ashamed. I have not abandoned you."

Amber tried to hold back her tears, but her eyes stung and the words were so comforting.

"Don't be scared, Amber. Fear cripples. Fear of death, loss, or judgment is all the same. Just know there is no room for fear in my love. Now, take my hand."

———

Amber awoke with a start. The image slid away like sand through the receding tide. The dream had ended.

Wet with sweat from her heavy sleep, she rose from the mattress and knelt on the stained rug beside her bed. Words rushed once again, and the sincerity of her prayer compelled her overwhelmed spirit to respond. "Please forgive me, Jesus. I've been wronged and hurt, but I've wronged and hurt you. I'm a sinner and I'm sorry. I want new life. Please help me. I need you and I love you."

Pulling her blanket and pillow from the floor, Amber nestled into a ball. Peering into the shadows surrounding the room, the darkness seemed lighter. The path clearer.

She prayed softly. "I'm scared Jesus. Show me the way home.

10

Another empty night. Crumbs from the late supper of chicken fingers and French fries lay scattered across the ring-stained coffee table. Sighing deeply, Amber eased back into the couch. The television flickered with an old cartoon she had seen at least three times. Gazing at the ceiling, she let her mind wander.

Memories were uneasy strangers to Amber. She remembered what she did not care to recall and forgot what she desperately longed to keep. But on this day, without fanfare, a distant moment returned unexpectedly.

Shortly after the hot, humid days of a Kansas summer they would appear. The cicada shells, clinging to the oak trees by the creek, invited even the most reluctant to pluck them from the bark. The children would whisper and laugh as they carefully detached the fragile skeletons, cradling them like precious treasures in the hollow of their hands. Then running along the banks, they would carry them as close to home as they could until they stumbled or crushed them. And Amber remembered the disappointment as she opened her hands and watched the wind carry the pieces falling to the stream below the bank.

One night as she sat on the front steps, she'd asked her father, "Are they magic?"

Her father had looked at her from the porch swing. "The tree crickets? No," he chuckled. "It's nature. You don't see them but it's their song you hear in the cool of the night."

Amber had come over to rock slowly with him, sliding her hand over his and he held hers and together they listened to the buzzing of the tree crickets.

"They burrow out of the ground and climb to the trees. Those shells are their childhood skin they leave behind. They emerge, and their music begins. Some say they sing for the memory of living underground."

Opening her eyes, Amber glanced at the television. Was she like that? Did she have a song? Or was she just an empty husk?

Earlier that evening, standing on the corner the man named Jackson had approached her and motioned to step into the alley, assumedly to talk "business." He gave his name, but Amber knew enough to know it wasn't his real name. He seemed normal, upon first glance, but judging character was a skill of survival for her and she could read people, especially men. There was something sinister in his eyes. He wanted to hurt her. She sensed it.

She searched the street for Big George.

Where is that fat man when you need him? she'd thought.

"Hey baby, I have a proposition for you," the john had said.

Not wanting to create a scene, Amber tried to ignore him, but her instincts said run. So she started walking away. Fast.

Jackson had blocked her and forced her down the dark alley, casting his eyes as if looking for someone. Clarity seized Amber then like the moment of waking from a dream. She knew what to do. Without another thought, she reached into her purse and pulled out the switchblade Big George had given her.

"For emergencies only, baby."

I guess this is it, she'd thought.

"Come here, you . . ." Instantly he was upon her. Clasping her shoulders he pushed her against the wall, then his fingers went to her neck constricting her throat. Summoning every ounce of strength in her small frame she tried to scream, but her lungs couldn't push the sound out.

"I'm gonna kill you, you little slut," he spit.

He tightened his grip on her, protecting himself from her thrashing by turning sideways. Time slowed down and her natural instincts kicked in. She swung the blade.

A scream of pain and tearing and blood and Amber looked in disbelief at the scene in front of her.

Clutching his side, he'd whined like a child. "You cut me . . ." then slumped to his knees as he groped in the darkness.

Even now, looking back, the details remained blurry. She ran from the alley and stumbled into Big George charging down the street. Sobbing, she fell into his arms and he motioned for another girl, Sugar, to take her to her apartment. Instantly, two of Big George's boys flew down the alley and she heard the screams echoing across the street, and then Big George's voice.

"Looks like my Misty got you good. Don't ever touch one of my girls again. Ever." And then the screams ended.

After the adrenaline had gone, Amber crumpled. Sugar got her inside but quickly returned to her post.

Why me? Amber thought. *Is this what's going to come of me? Will I just be killed one day at the hands of a crazy man? How can I wake from this horrible dream?*

Suddenly, ragged anger tore through her veins like acid erupting from a pipe. She wanted to destroy something. To hurt someone. To punish everyone who had inflicted daily misery on her and her body.

But even more, she wanted to punish herself for staying here.

Rolling over, she screamed into a throw pillow.

"I hate you! *I! hate! yooou!*" Though she meant herself.

"So why do you stay, Amber? Huh? Why. Do. You. Stay?"

Yes. Run.

"No. They'd kill me."

No. You could kill them.

Instantly the words stopped her. A sharp realization coursed through her mind.

She could. She could kill them all while they slept. She pulled in her knees, recoiling from the thought and her hands shook like a drunk's. The echo of her own thoughts returned to her ears and she started to cry.

She knew she couldn't do it. But there was a part of her that wished she could.

No one cared. She was completely, utterly, alone.

Oblivious to her surroundings, tormenting only herself, Amber tossed and turned on the couch, struggling for peace.

"Please, God!" Amber begged. *"Please let me disappear."*

———

Amber awoke to the morning sun beginning its relentless creep over the horizon. Climbing from the earthen hollow, she stretched her arms wishing she could embrace the warmth of the light. The sound of crunching earth behind her startled her and she quickly turned.

"Sorry about that, Amber. I didn't mean to scare you." His voice was so soothing.

"That's okay, Jesus," Amber nervously laughed. "Sometimes, I scare myself just burping."

Jesus threw back his head and laughed. "Ha ha! And I've heard you burp! It is scary!"

Amber smiled.

"You've had a tough day." He stopped a couple feet in front of her and lowered his head. "Wanna talk about it?"

"I'm spitting mad, actually. I hate my life, which isn't even mine. I'm a sex slave who people treat like garbage. Worse than garbage! And the feelings are killing me. I just want to kill them. But mostly I just want out of this mess."

"You may not believe this, but I understand," Jesus responded. "I've been there. I remember a time I got so upset I started throwing tables and chairs."

Amber sniffed and wiped her eyes. "I remember that." She plopped down on the soft grass and motioned for Jesus to sit down. "Would you tell me about it? Please?"

"Well," Jesus began, "for me it was about what men were doing to my most sacred place. It was very much like what you're feeling. You should be angry about what they are doing to you. I certainly am."

"You are." Amber stated it more as a confirmation than a question. She'd always believed Jesus was kind and good. But she'd never thought of what he felt when people hurt each other. "I get so mad, I want to break things."

"I know. But that's not the point."

"Well, what is the point?" Amber quizzed.

"You want to teach them a lesson?"

"Is that what you were doing?" Amber asked.

"The temple was God's house, the only place people believed he actually lived on earth.

Very different from how it is now. Now, God makes his home in you, in your heart. When I come in, your body is the temple."

"I'm sorry." Amber shook her head befuddled. "That's just words to me."

"Your body is fingers, hands, a torso, legs, feet, head."

"Right."

"The temple court had many parts. They were using it for cheating people and making money. Trashing my Father's house. I couldn't help myself. My rage came from this place within as I thought of them making people pay to get to God and making them miss him entirely. So I drove them out. I was overturning tables, but I was trying to overturn their system, all the things they thought of as precious 'valuables' spilled and scattered. People don't respect God's wrath. They don't understand how it's a fact of his love."

Amber looked at Jesus' deep blue eyes and again slowly shook her head. "No."

"It was empty religion." Jesus went on. "A show. They were making light of the most sacred. That's a huge reason why I came. To abolish religion from the inside out. I wanted people to see you have to change from the inside out." Pausing, he caught her looking away, "You want me to go on?"

"Yeah, go ahead," Amber said. "I was just thinking how that's exactly what I've wanted for so long."

"Mmm . . ." Jesus stopped and glanced around. "Hold on a sec."

He pushed himself up on his knees and tromped over to grab a rock, then another and another. Puzzled, Amber watched as Jesus zigzagged around the field. He returned and squatted in front her.

74

"Remember stacking blocks when you were a kid?" He pulled various size rocks from his hat which had served as a bucket and began setting them up in a mound.

"Sure."

"Did it make you mad when your brother knocked them down?"

"You know it did," Amber said remembering. "Ohh! That made me so mad."

"Now," he said, carefully placing the final rock on the pile. "Knock it down."

Amber looked up at him. "You want me to?"

"You don't?"

"I don't know," Amber said, "It feels wrong somehow."

"Why?" Jesus pressed.

Amber shrugged. "I guess. Since you told me to . . ."

"It's different when I ask you to?"

"Versus if you didn't? Yeah."

Laughter escaped from him again. Then he nodded and smiled.

Her hand swung and the rocks flew.

"Whoa! You are crazy strong," Jesus laughed again. "Just about took my head off!"

"Sorry."

"Felt good, huh?"

"Yeah. It did." And then she paused. "It was like . . . I was doing what you asked."

"Exactly how it felt for me. God asked, I did it. So it was all good."

A silence passed between them and then finally Jesus said, "Can I show you something else?"

"Sure." Amber smiled. "Do I get to knock stuff down?"

"Ha! I want to show you how the body is like a temple."

"Okay." Though she knew better, something in her prepared to hurt. Maybe he wouldn't mention her specifically.

"Everyone has flesh and blood, bone and muscle." Jesus twisted two stalks of grass together between his hands. "But there's also a soul, like the inner court in the temple. In my time, it was reserved for the priest. Only the ceremonial sanctified could enter it."

Amber thought back to her home church and recalled the altar at the front waiting for people to dedicate themselves or receive prayer.

"So when I cleared the temple courts I made it clear they were next!"

Amber smiled. "You were coming for them!"

Jesus laughed. "So true, Amber. So true. But that was part of my work. To reveal dead religion. And rock the system of getting to God."

Amber was liking this. She leaned back into the high grass.

"But here's the thing. Every human being, has an inner court. And religion with all its rules, well, it tries to soothe the guilty conscience and it can't work. No rule can remove the stain that makes you feel dirty. No law can comfort a broken heart or make someone love. Every person must take responsibility for their own inner court and decide what they're going to let in—law or love." He watched her to see if she was getting it and Jesus pressed on. "For within the soul, there is a part you call the spirit, and that's like the holy of holies. You've heard of that?"

Amber quietly nodded. "Basically the center of the inner court. Crazy special. Like drop dead if you aren't worthy."

Jesus pointed at her. "You were listening! Yes. It's where God's actual presence was said to reside on the earth. God made sure people respected this place."

"Destroy this temple, and I will raise it again in three days."

Jesus cracked a wry smile. "Now you're getting ahead of me. Exactly. The old way of doing things would soon be forever changed. No more sacrifices. No more temple tax."

76

"New sheriff in town," Amber said.

"Life is, and always will be, about nothing more than faith in a God who sent His Son to offer a way to get clean forever."

"It's amazing," Amber said and then rose to her feet. "I know you don't have to be here with me, but you are. I want to believe, I do. But I'm a mess."

"Don't say that, Amber. I know our time is limited here, but don't cut yourself down. Your situation is rough. And you're really trying."

"Yeah. Just being here with you now, that's enough for me."

Jesus stood. "See you soon, my friend."

"Yes, you will Jesus. I got loads more stuff to talk about."

"I'm always here."

The image faded and cracking her eyes open, Amber awoke with the television playing softly in the background. Shifting on the stained couch, hunger crept into her gut. Rising she moved to the cabinet. Grabbing peanut butter and crackers she stood silently at the counter. Dipping the cracker she attempted loading the peanut butter but managed only to break the cracker. Disgusted she turned, angry at the failure of even the simplest task. Pausing, she abruptly stopped, pulled open a drawer, and grabbed a spoon. Thrusting it harshly into the peanut butter she pulled out a heaping mound and crammed it into her mouth. Nutty flavor coursed through her taste buds and she quickly swallowed and then repeated. Like the explosion of a filament light bulb fracturing in its socket, she understood. *The only escape is to go all out. No dabbling.*

11

"Dang you, dumb cop," Carey exclaimed as his coffee spilled over the edge of his Kwiktrip cup and plopped onto his iPad.

"Are you kidding me?" He wiped frantically. "Great. Ruining government property and talking to yourself."

Vice Detective Carey Mueller set the tablet aside, stuck his cup in the holder and blotted at the coffee on his pants, trying not to think about the emails that'd be waiting for him after his shift. Another worthless evening spent watching the druggies, prostitutes and pimps trolling West Street.

"What am I doing here?" he asked the windshield. "Stop one fight, one deal, won't change a stinkin' thing."

His eyes slipped to a young blonde girl strutting her stuff.

"There. Reason number two. Big George's system. He doesn't give a crap; she doesn't give a crap. Charging anyone dumb enough to need it."

Like a warning shot across the bow of a ship, a black Lexus sidled up beside Sugar. She stopped and leaned at the waist into the passenger's window. Carey couldn't hear the conversation, but he knew the words, the song and dance of the scenario that would play out with or without him watching.

Moments later, she stepped into the car and it pulled slowly back into traffic.

"Freakin 2:00 am business is booming." Carey sipped and his thoughts turned to the girl left on the sidewalk. The dark-haired one in the white jacket. He hadn't noticed her before, standing huddled in the alcove of the old tool shop.

What was she doing? George made his walkers walk.

What if you could save just one?

Carey knew the voice was in his head, but he looked around the cruiser anyway. Now he knew he was going crazy.

But the idea had legs. "Not just lock one up, but save one?"

He chuckled. It was idiotic. It wouldn't change jack.

"Good Lord," he sighed. "You are losing it, bro!"

Later, as Carey showered after his shift and succumbed to the idea in the privacy of his home, he would describe it to his wife as "one of those emotional moments when you lost your head and fell into stupid world."

How in the world could he hope to make a difference—even for one? Honestly, he was just lint in the pages of history. With a mouth full of water he whispered the words, "I, Carey James Mueller couldn't make a difference if opportunity stepped up and slapped me in the face."

He dressed for his men's group and said goodbye to his wife and daughter and drove to the coffee bar. Demoralized, perplexed and slightly nervous, he mentioned the subject to the guys.

"I don't know why it's hitting me like this," he said. "You think someone's trying to tell me something?"

"I can't see why not," his friend said.

After batting it around a while, the general consensus was he should at least be open to the notion that helping someone was what he became a cop for. Someone proposed that, "anyone can wall themselves off, pretend the world doesn't exist but in their little bubble, and try to muddle on through life. But a man steps up and attempts to change someone's life."

Carey had to concede the point.

"Listen," Michael the group leader said. "It's the parable of the lost sheep in Luke 15." He pulled out his phone and summoned the passage. "How glad they will be in heaven over one sinner who repents—more than over ninety-nine righteous people who don't need repentance."

They talked some more and others shared, but Carey still felt compelled to apologize for making it all about him. "Didn't mean to commandeer the vehicle tonight, guys," he said.

"You didn't, bro. Can we pray for you?" Michael asked and Carey nodded, asking God to show him the "one single life" he was to help.

Walking to his car, Carey felt the buzz of an incoming call. Looking at the number, he chuckled, "Murray Jackson."

"Hey, bro! What's doin' in Gilroy?"

"Usual. Cow-tipping and assorted shenanigans. What about you, big city man?"

Carey sighed. "I don't suppose you know of any lost sheep I might rescue."

"Well . . . Okay, this is weird. But you're Det Mueller so you're used to weird."

"Shoot."

"Guy named Ray Ellis might give you a call. He's looking for help finding his daughter who was kidnapped six years ago. Thinks she's there in Chicago."

"Wow. Okay." Carey felt a shiver trail his spine but said nothing. "I'll keep my cell on."

"Thanks, Carey."

"Anytime. Thanks for calling."

"Be safe, bro."

"Take it easy, Murray."

Throwing his phone on the passenger seat, Carey started the car and pulled out, feelings from the earlier evening's conversation with himself rumbling through his chest. A horn blast jolted him back to reality and he fumbled with the wheel, narrowly avoiding another car.

"Get off the street, moron!" screamed the driver.

Carey managed a weak wave and mouthed, "I'm sorry."

Sighing again, he finished with a chuckle. "Yep, that's my problem. Too long on the streets." Looking upward he quickly prayed, "Help me God. Let me find that one lost sheep."

12

Amber woke to the sound of tree crickets singing in the night.

She opened her eyes and rolled over. Nope. Just the space heater.

Notes of a song wafted silently through the darkness, a music more felt than heard, but yet unrecognized. Was the truth that she was just an empty husk clinging to the bark of a forgotten tree? Would she just slip away in the dark? And if she did, what would she be left holding in her hand?

Daylight was to Amber what it was to the nocturnal creatures. She slept when the world awoke, walking while the good people curled up in their beds. Sleep for her was an elusive spider scurrying across the floor. A creepy intruder she didn't want to catch. But necessity demanded it.

She sat up. No longer coveting her drugs or her music, Amber now eagerly pulled the little black book of *John* from under her mattress and began reading.

Funny. If someone would have told her she'd read the Bible like this, hoping to see Jesus again in her dreams, she might have mumbled filthy words and laughed. Why would Jesus even want to talk to her? The thought was beyond comprehension. But the routine was the same, night after night.

Her eyes heavy with exhaustion, the words soon began to swim in endless liquid shapes in front of her face. Her head sunk to her chest and daylight faded to blackness.

————

Amber cracked open her eyes expecting to see the familiar tall grass of the field. Instead, she found herself in an old Victorian parlor with floor to ceiling curtains, high-backed velvet chairs and rich paintings adorning every wall. Mahogany wood dark as if it were painted black cast an opaque curtain that obscured her memory. Like heavy dust upon a frosted window she scrubbed her mind searching for anything to recall where she might be.

Several moments passed and then, like butter melting on hot bread, she remembered. The parlor looked strangely like her Aunt Winnie's. She had loved her occasional visit to Aunt Winnie's, her father's oldest sister. She'd lived in Jewell, Kansas, about two hours from them, and the entire family had looked forward to the visits. The stately home where Aunt Winnie lived alone was one of the most beautiful places on earth. Aunt Winnie had greeted them at the door and ushered them in with hugs and a flurry of excitement, and then shortly after arrival a small bell had ting-a-linged and a maid announced, "Tea is served."

The memory flooded her now as one of the best afternoons of her life, sipping tea and nibbling cookies while Aunt Winnie peppered her with questions about her life.

"I took so much for granted," she thought. For that hour, she had been the center of someone's universe.

And to this very moment, she'd forgotten having ever felt such peace. But with its return arose a rekindled sense of purpose.

A whisper announced his entrance, and in a moment, even in the low-lit room, Amber felt the change. His walk was familiar as he crossed the room to her. "Hello, Amber. It's nice to see you again."

All fear and anxiety were now buried memories, and she jumped to her feet and toward him. A momentary doubt flicked through her—*Maybe he was angry with her? Had he come to scold her?*—but from her heart, the truth traveled to her mind, and Amber knew he had come to love her.

He was here for her, to visit with *her!*

Customary greetings forgotten, Amber wrapped her arms around him and he fell back slightly, laughing, hugging her back. And the soothing words he spoke to her left no simple interpretation.

"There. Everything is fine. I am here."

After several moments, she recalled her question for him. "Jesus," she stood back from him just a bit. "I need to understand your visit with the woman at the well."

He stepped back more and looked at her. Great empathy etched his face, as though he had sensed this coming for a while. Slowly he meandered to the high-back chair and sat. The red velvet matched his flannel work shirt. Laying his head back, Jesus sighed.

"This is nice, very comfortable."

"Well," responded Amber. Her eyes blazed with intensity and her hands flew to her hips striking a pose of indignation. "You know why I need to understand that story . . ."

"I do." Jesus pointed no finger, no retort, only the same look of love. "Well. I was thirsty. Honestly, that's all it was." Jesus laughed and said, "People sometimes forget that. I got thirsty. But . . ." he continued after a pause, "once I saw her, I knew she had a lot going on. You know what I mean?"

Amber smiled and perched on the lip of her chair.

"She was so transparent—and I was skeptical."

"Skeptical?"

"I said, 'If you knew the gift of God, who it is that asks you for a drink, you would have asked him and he would have given you living water.' By her response, I could see she was curious and maybe she'd heard of me. But her heart was a minefield. I'd have to cross it because she was on the other side.

"Like me? Turning her head as if talking to herself, she mumbled barely coherent. "The fear cripples me and I can't move. I just stand there. Frozen."

Jesus stiffened and answered. "Yes! And she was clever like you. She tried to avoid me first with cynicism and sarcasm. Tools she'd used for years."

Amber dropped her eyes.

Acknowledging Amber's reaction, Jesus continued. "She'd figured out who I was. Thought she knew me, from what she'd heard. 'Well, sir,' she said, 'you have nothing to draw with. And this well is deep. How will you get this living water? You think you're greater than our father Jacob who gave us this well?'"

"She was making fun of you" Amber shifted on the chair.

"Sorta. She was saying, 'Prove it, Jesus.' Sarcasm is a shield to protect against disappointment. She'd learned to expect it." He nodded at her. "I know you relate to that."

Amber nodded too. "But you stepped around the mine."

"I didn't answer her directly. I just moved on."

"Everyone who drinks this water will get thirsty again. But if you drink the water I give, you won't ever be thirsty again. This water will become your own personal spring gushing fountains of eternal life."

"And she wanted it." Amber leaned forward.

"Not yet," Jesus smiled.

"After a couple of moments, she said, 'Then give me this living water so I won't have to keep coming here.'"

"Was she still skeptical?"

"You remember playing chess?"

Amber laughed. "Yeah. I stink at it."

"It's tough playing against the computer, right? You can never win."

Amber stared intently into his eyes, his emotion revealing itself like a ray of light. His eyes almost glowed. Amber saw nothing unusual, yet everything about him was unique.

His passion was contagious.

"I knew I had her then," he said.

"That's when you said, 'Go, call your husband and come back.'"

"Yes," Jesus quietly replied. "I knew she was taking a terrible risk talking to me without her husband. So I figured, let's get this out in the open."

"And that's when she said, 'I don't have a husband.'"

"I looked at her, just like I'm looking at you now, and I said, 'You're right about that because you've had five, and the man you're with now isn't your husband.' And her cynicism just drained away. The fire fled from her eyes and she asked if I was a prophet and proceeded to tell me why she could never follow me because of her heritage. I just kept looking at her, like this. Never, had she been offered kindness, let alone forgiveness. Not even once."

Amber felt his penetrating gaze and reached into the back pocket of her jeans and pulled out the little black book she had found on the street. She turned to the place and began reading. "Believe me, the time is coming when you won't worship on this mountain or Jerusalem. You worship what you don't know. We worship what we do know; salvation is indeed from the Jews. But the time is coming—indeed, it's here already!—when true worshipers will worship God in spirit and truth. Yes: that's the kind of worshipers he's looking for."

Jesus's voice joined hers. "God is spirit, and those who worship him must worship in spirit and truth."

Then Amber's voice alone again. "I know that Messiah is coming," said the woman, "the one they call 'the anointed.' When he comes, he tells us everything."

Then Jesus declared the words as she read them, "I am he—the one speaking to you right now."

Amber looked up at him and tears slid down her cheeks and to her lip.

His eyes locked on her and again he smiled. Amber weakly smiled back and wiped the pages. She whispered it again.

"I am he—the one speaking to you right now."

13

Ray shaved and threw on an old pair of jeans and a Kansas City Royals shirt that had seen better days. Something new was in the air this morning. Grabbing a cup of coffee, he jumped in his truck and drove to the Alpine County Sheriff's office. Sheriff Murray T. Jackson had been in the Sheriff's office for the past sixteen years and knew forward and backward the sad search for Amber and Meghan. He had been there every step of the way for Ray's family and Ray had appreciated the concern.

"Hi, Ray," Sheriff Jackson yelled as the battered door to the office jangled open. "How you doing, old friend?"

"Eh. You know." Ray's voice wavered as the memories of distant hours and days passed in this office bore down on him like a Kansas wind roaring through the prairie grass. Clouds of dust swirled on the open field of Ray's mind and blew it to a place and feeling he had long since repressed. The anguish, the shame, and the loss were all reignited, this time with a new desperation burning itself into the desolate floor of his heart.

"Not so good, huh?" Sheriff Murray said, watching Ray's face.

"Yeah." Ray hoped the weakness he felt wasn't noticeable in his face. "How can I help?"

Ray swallowed and plunged in. "Yesterday I overheard Marc Gooden talking about the arrest of Junior Holler and Elliott Watts."

There. He had said it out loud. *It felt good to associate actual names with the disappearance of Amber and Meghan.* No one, not even Meghan's mother who'd left over two years ago, ever hoped to find something so tangible as this lead.

Murray's eyes widened and his bright smile faded like steam rising off dampened turf.

"Oh man, Ray."

"I know—" Ray began.

"Listen, there's no confirmation they were even active at the time of Amber and Meghan's abduction."

"Murray! I'm sick with this thing." Softening his voice, Ray said it again more for himself and less for Murray. "I'm sick with this thing. It's been six years and I can't go on with no answers and no hope. I'm begging you, Murray. Give me a bone."

Desperation hung in the air. He could never take back all that had already been said between them, even if he'd wanted too. Ray knew he was pushing hard as a driving rain, but Murray had to feel Ray's pain. Sheriff Jackson blinked and after a moment of leaning back and regarding Ray, he replied in a carefully measured tone. "Okay, Ray. Let me make some calls and I'll get back to you with everything I find out."

Ray's breath caught. "Sheriff, that's—I appreciate it. Here's my new cell." Ray handed Sheriff Jackson a slip of paper. "You can reach me there."

"Going away?" Murray held his gaze like the experienced fisherman he was.

"I'm headed to Chicago to find Amber."

"By yourself." Sheriff Jackson asked incuriously.

"I have to go, Murray. I know it's a long shot but I've got to put up or shut up. I can't explain it but something is driving me to look one more time." He'd gone several years before for a few days but overwhelmed by the labyrinthine networks of underground clubs and brothels, and sensing himself in over his head, he'd given up. Pausing for breath, he added, "Call it a side effect of prolonged misery. Maybe it's the Holy Spirit. Maybe it was bad pizza. But I can't *not* do something. Surely, you understand that better than anyone."

Sheriff Murray stared intently into his face. He knew he sympathized and yet honestly, he could not comprehend what had worked its way into the fiber of Ray's bones. Could he deny a man seeking his life which had disappeared? Ray knew the loss of a child had physically and emotionally taken its toll and showed in his carriage. Once a picture of solidity and health, shades of gray now streaked Ray's wrinkled brow. Yet he knew his eyes must burn fiercely and so he stared back at Sheriff Jackson.

Choosing his words, Murray said, "I can appreciate your determination. I can. But listen. If I can't talk you out of this, at least let me call a friend who might be able to steer you in a particular direction. He's a vice cop in the 5th precinct on the south side. And you know the odds of finding Amber, but he'd know the rings running there. I'll let him know you're coming."

Ray's internal storm suddenly slackened and droplets began to twirl through the shadows. His darkened corner brightened, transforming Ray's fatigue and he smiled for the first time at Sheriff Jackson.

"Thanks, Sheriff." He took one of the Sheriff's up-turned hands and shook it, then turned quickly to walk across the checkered tile floor. The slap of his shoes echoed in the empty cellblocks with finality. He would leave Gilroy, the house—his brother would take care of it—and the store would be there when he returned, whenever that might be. He thanked God for the store that made enough for him to employ Mike as store manager and a couple reliable employees.

It was time.

"Hey, Ray?"

Ray glanced back.

"Be safe. And God bless you."

"Thanks, Murray. For everything."

Ray saw Sheriff Jackson blink back the moisture in his eyes, but left before the statement that punctuated the empty space he'd left.

"That poor man. That poor, sad man."

14

A duffel of clothes, assorted toiletries and a light jacket littered the front seat of Ray's pick-up. Balding tires hummed across hot pavement as the miles dropped endlessly behind. Stopping for gas and snack food, Ray willed his truck and his spirit forward.

He listened to sports on the radio to occupy his mind which would invariably wander and he dreaded facing the horrors that awaited him. Still, he knew he couldn't face the walking coma he'd lived. Moments would pass where Ray could step clear out of his thoughts, only to return some time later unaware of his surroundings, his hands tightly gripping the steering wheel. He knew he was in a dangerous spot. Not to mention, an extremely unhealthy place. Yet, like a cold sore lurking beneath the skin, he couldn't deny it was there and had to be faced. Whatever pain and anger at God, at men, at himself and at life came with this, he had to accept it.

It was real. The darkness he dreaded facing, it existed.

So for the first time in a long while, he prayed. He prayed not like before, but as though God was his only hope, pouring out his thoughts and spirit, desperate to release the torrents of pain and anguish that had been building inside him ever since he stopped reaching for the Mediator.

"Oh, God! I don't know what I'm doing. Your word says if we lack wisdom to ask and you will grant it. And I believe you're in this with me. And I need your help, Lord."

He sweated and prayed as he drove, the skyline of Chicago looming in the gray horizon. Sunlight was fading, night was dawning. Finally, he rolled down his window, pushing out a haggard breath and sucked in the dirty suburban air of Chicago.

"Time to find out what I'm made of."

Ray's Internet search had revealed the top prostitution hives were on E Street. That's where he'd decided to start.

He didn't know how long he could last without any clues, but he hoped at least longer than last time. Still, considering the toll it had taken before, he knew time was short; every day counted. His resolve wouldn't quit this time, but his mind and body might. He was too close to the edge. Sleep and food were a necessary waste of time.

Straining to quell the boiling in his blood, Ray drove to the first place the computer had revealed. The lights on E street blazed with depictions of services available: NUDE GIRLS. XXX. TOPLESS. Sickened by the brazenness of it all, Ray parked his truck, again prayed for Holy Spirit wisdom and control, and crossed the wide street.

Brushing aside the beaded curtain, Ray moved into a darkened room. Allowing his dilated pupils to refocus he surveyed the setting. The room was lined with black walnut paneling, and sconces of glass hung oddly on the walls, as an afterthought. Shaggy, multi-colored carpeting looked like a breeding ground for various insects. A vaguely familiar Pet Shop Boys song coursed through tiny speakers from the corners and Ray's nostrils pinched in the stench of *eau de old building* covered in cheap perfume and rotten beef jerky. The entire scene was like going back in time to the early 90s. With nods to the 70s.

Do people still go for this? Ray haltingly thought. Seeing no one, he assumed not many. He stood in the fluorescent-lit shop and slowly, the atmosphere grew more familiar and the old music became more noticeable.

What have I done to deserve this? the song pled.

Ray sensed himself identifying.

Get a grip, man.

"Hey, baby," a scantily clad, smoky-voiced blonde emerged from the inner doorway. She couldn't have been more than twenty years old.

"What does Papa want tonight?" She placed a soft hand on his arm.

"Nothing," Ray bristled. "Just need to talk to the manager."

Scoffing, she sauntered away to greet a man stepping through the beaded curtain.

"You have no idea what you're missing, Pops."

Ray swallowed hard and thought to himself, *Thank goodness for that.*

Without thinking, Ray bolted for the side door. Reaching his truck he gripped the door handle and stopped. Seeing his reflection, he considered the man staring back. Ashen, sunken-eyes, the picture cast a passing resemblance to a man he'd once known. Rubbing his eyes, he regarded the apparition.

You've seen this before, he told it. *You remember this feeling. You've felt loneliness plenty. But you're older now and you know how it works. A woman's tenderness is not something you're owed. It's earned through sacrifice and commitment.*

He knew how easy it would be to believe the lie, of course. And nobody would ever know. But these women were all someone's daughters. Someone's potential wives.

The sudden ache of missing his wife's hand on his arm caused a shudder to ripple through him and he suddenly felt the fatigue of the long drive.

Ray stood across the street watching the patrons shuffle in and out of the brothel. Faces traced with fear, others with shame, each thinking only of where they had to be. Each in captivity to their bodies and the faithless fear—*"How am I gonna get through?"*

"Where in the world are the cops?" Ray wondered. *"Doesn't anyone care God?"*

———

Across the street, unaware of Ray's presence, Detective Carey Mueller sat in his unmarked patrol car wondering how men of position and influence and those with little means could all be bewitched. How could each one march so mindlessly into momentary satisfaction? Like buffalo following the herd, they soared off the cliff into a future of more pain and loss.

Some would even experience the walking death. He knew that all too well.

Instead of relief from their loneliness, they were only becoming part of the cause. They would perpetuate the lies and waste everything on ever more selfish promises of happiness. And what would be the result? Carey knew. Broken relationships would be the outcome. Betrayal was betrayal, and it always brought fresh wounds whether or not they wanted to admit it. The prize in the end would be only a strengthened and more unquenchable lust.

The walking death. Self-respect and chivalry dissolved. He had seen it a hundred times before, even experienced it himself. Yet it never ceased. Generation after generation. Civilization after civilization. Father to son to grandson.

Where was the grand love, the extraordinary? What was the cause of all this evil?

Sin. Carey thought. *Plain, common, ugly sin.*

15

Ray quickly brushed his teeth, smashed warm water over his face and stumbled into bed. The stinking hotel room suddenly made him gag and he rolled over to smother his face in his sheets and pillow wishing for a breath of fresh country air.

Does she miss the clean air of the farm? Ray mused. He had to believe she was out there and all this was worth it. And mercifully, somehow, he did. Thoughts of his family rolled through his mind, and closing his eyes, he offered a short prayer for each.

Within minutes, exhaustion dragged through his bones and he slept.

When the midmorning sun splashed through the thin curtains, he groaned and through bleary eyes peered at the water-stained ceiling. Frustrated by his immediate thoughts of giving up and going back home, he slipped to his knees on the scratchy, nap-worn carpet and began to pray.

"Father I need your guidance. Help me to find her. When I meet with Detective Mueller today, let him understand. I need help, Lord Jesus. But, I can't do this by myself."

He looked around. Only God knew what trials and trespasses it had seen. "Life gets you dirty, huh?" he muttered. Grabbing his jacket and keys he paused at the door. "I need you Lord. Give me strength today."

———

The sound of traffic melted into the thumping bumping bustle of another day on the streets of south Chicago. What started as a wander through the streets of the south side prostitution houses was beginning to resemble a muddle through twisted shops and snarled back alleys. Endless winding streets, corner after corner, and multiple alleyways blurred together. Within an hour and a half, Ray was utterly, totally at a loss.

"This sure ain't Kansas anymore," he mumbled, studying his folded map and staring at endless rows of shops and acres of concrete.

"Nope. It's Southside Chicago, farmer man!"

Determining the voice was different than the one in his head, Ray turned around to see a scraggy twenty-something man leaning against a convenience store wall smoking a cigarette. His pants sagged and his white cap was on sideways. Ray tried not to give away his fear.

"Yep," he responded lamely.

"What street you looking for?"

"Oh, no worries," he half-shouted, turning back around and pushing the potential words for this situation from his mind. *Robbery. Assault and battery. Shakedown.*

"Whatever, man."

100

Plunging down the sidewalk, Ray made to escape. But a peaceful assurance stopped him and a question popped into his head. He turned back.

"Can I ask you something?"

The guy lifted his chin.

"What's your name?"

"Griz."

"Griz."

"I really look like a farmer?"

The young man snorted and flicked his cigarette. "Naw, Old MacDonald. You look good."

Ray smiled and looked down at his boots. "I was afraid of that. Any advice?"

Did he just ask a gang-banger for advice?

"You ain't no cop?"

"No. I'm a Christian."

Griz scoffed and then regarded him seriously. "You think you gonna save some people?"

"Maybe. Actually. Just one. I'm gonna try." He did sound like Old MacDonald!

"I'm looking for someone. Her name is Amber." Griz's face hardened and Ray knew instantly he had made a mistake. A big one. Ray flushed self-consciously. He couldn't help himself.

What am I doing? What if this is one of those street narcs that reports everything to some big boss. Good grief. I watch too much television.

Griz made a face and waved him off. Ray turned to the sidewalk and strode forward, not much of a better notion of where he was headed than before. Behind him the young man called. "Hey, Christian."

Ray turned.

"Ain't nothing you can do. You watch yourself out there."

———

He found a quiet spot in the *Café Espresso* to get better bearings and feel safer pulling out his phone. He'd found an app that could age a photo and he scanned in the last picture of Amber he had, adding six years. In moments, Ray was staring at a twenty-year-old Amber. The resemblance to his wife Amanda was startling. His baby girl was now a beautiful woman and his heart hammered with regret for the time he'd lost and for the girl and the wife he still loved.

It was 10:15. He wasn't supposed to meet Carey here until 3:00. So he decided to go make some inquiries. Like a pesky drunk, Ray staggered from vendor to stoop to bus stop to shop, shoving the phone under dozens of noses. "Have you seen this girl?" He soldiered on ignoring the perplexed looks, the curses and indifference, but within hours, they'd brought him to his knees.

He sunk to the steps of a nondescript brick apartment building on E Street in downtown Chicago as a piece of crumpled paper rose into the smoggy sky. His head in his hands, ignorant to the stares and laughter of bystanders, Ray groaned. "This is insane."

He peered down the street. Dozens of people flowed along the avenue, strangers meandering from point to point, oblivious to the immortality in their souls. Trapped in a glass, unaware, they relentlessly pursued whatever propelled them. Invisible forces seemed to manipulate them into their strict paths, pressing them forward out of compliance.

How long had he done the same, never questioning the expected routine day after day, pretending everything was just fine?

Ray coughed and wished for a breath mint or a stick of gum. Something, anything to banish the film coating his tongue. But what would clean his mind and heart?

"Jesus, show me where to go. What do I do?"

Silence surrounded him though the sea of tumult continued flowing by unabated. The afternoon sun was slipping over the buildings. Thrusting his face upward to catch the full glance of the sun, peacefulness descended again into his spirit. He opened his eyes and looked across the street.

There.

The sign flashed "24 HOURS XXX ADULT." He breathed and smiled to heaven. "Thank you, God." He rejoined his quest, cautiously moving across the street.

Entering the small shop, he felt prepared. No wavering this time, no temptation, no lapse. Every woman here represented someone's loved daughter, sister, mother or future grandmother. Each silent figure wanted true love and acceptance. And there was no "magic" awaiting anyone here. Just a lie that had stolen all of them and his own child.

Maybe Griz was right—he could do nothing about the cycle. But maybe he could save one girl out of it.

Maybe. And as long as that existed, he would not be altered. His daughter lived. He knew it as surely now as he knew he would never stop looking. He was a man born anew, determined to right what had been wronged, regardless of what he might face.

The neon arrow pointed to an obscure doorway angling around the side of the white brick and blue-trimmed building. Throwing caution aside, Ray abruptly stepped inside. Plastic DVD boxes lined multiple rows of wire racks. Posters of products and mannequins in lingerie lined the walls and flashing lights announced the assorted sundries and promises of fulfillment. Printed-paper banners blazed trails to the deeper interior.

At the counter, a bearded man stared intently into the screen of a computer. Measuring his words and his steps, Ray moved guardedly forward.

"Can I help you, buddy?" the man said without glancing up.

"Uh, yes. I was wondering if you had seen this girl?"

"DVD or magazine?"

Puzzled, Ray replied, "Uh, neither."

"Live stuff's next door." Receiving no reply, his eyes suddenly flicked up and measured Ray. "First time?"

"I'm sorry?"

"Good Lord, man, you a virgin?"

"Uhh . . . no." Ray blushed.

The man's eyes traveled over Ray. "You look lost," he said. "Got it bad for her huh? Okay. Okay. Let me see."

Silently Ray held up the phone.

"That's an altered photo. What's her name?"

"Amber," Ray quickly said. Ragged breath pushed out and his heart pounded like a meaty fist across his chest.

"No, stupid. Her stage name. Artist name."

"I . . . Just Amber."

Without warning the man's eyes flared and with one swift motion his right hand flashed across the desk and gripped Ray's hand crushing it like a vise.

"Are you a freak?" he breathed close to Ray's cringing face.

Years of farm and hardware store work had toughened Ray but he was unprepared for the violence, the rage from this stranger.

"No! I'm . . . her father!"

Quicker than the outburst, the release was even more furious.

"Okay, get out. Who the hell do you think you are, man?" he spat.

"Just a father looking for his daughter."

Snorting, the man whipped toward the door, "Out or I call the cops."

"Please." Ray's knees suddenly felt weak but he willed himself to stay put.

The man went for the phone and a moment of silence passed. Then he put it back on the receiver. "Okay, man. But listen, I'm not helping you," he mumbled.

Ray nodded.

The man looked at the phone in Ray's hand again. "She's not familiar. She's probably a walker."

"A walker?"

"Yeah. Like, she turns tricks on the street." Seeing the confusion on Ray's face, he asked, "You comprendo?"

Ray's heart sank like a stone and landed in a deep crevice. "Yes. Yes. I understand."

"And now you need to leave."

Ray nodded. "Thank you." The man held up his hands and Ray moved to the exit.

Outside, the bright Chicago sky disoriented Ray's senses and stumbling around the backside of the building he bent over and vomited the tension and fear from his body. Deep wretches racked his frame as the realization overtook his heart and mind.

A prostitute?

He heaved again.

What did I expect?

Wiping his mouth, he returned to E Street.

Summoning an inner strength he had not yet accessed, Ray stiffened, adjusted his shirt and forced himself back to the café.

Time to man up, Ray. Time to man up.

———

From across the street, a big man in a black hoodie and dark sunglasses pulled a cell phone from his pocket. "Call boss," he said.

"Calling boss," replied the phone.

The man put the phone to his ear and followed Ray at a distance. "Yeah, boss? We might have a problem."

16.

"Hey!"

Ray turned to see a short man in a black hoodie saunter toward him. Three figures slinked behind him and Ray's senses went on full alert.

"What are you doin'? You lost? What's your name?" The assault of questions continued.

Defiance rose quickly in Ray. "Who wants to know?"

"I'm asking the questions," the hooded one replied. Like shadows, the henchmen suddenly cornered Ray. Unable to run, he found himself dragged against his will down a dark abandoned alley.

"Now, like I said. Who are you?"

Ray realized the situation and the defiance faded as fear thundered down upon him like a sudden hailstorm. He was in trouble. Big trouble. Why hadn't he just stayed in the café?

"My name is Ray."

"Ray what?" The dark leader slowly said as if savoring the sound. Had the kid at the convenience store tipped them off?

"Ray. Just Ray."

"Okay Ray Just-Ray. What you looking for in our neighborhood?" Laughing, he flicked the ash off his half-smoked cigarette onto Ray's shoes.

"My daughter," Ray steely replied. No matter what he faced, he could not contain his passion for his quest. It guided him and exuded from his every pore.

"Oh, really. What's her name?"

"Amber."

The man just stared.

"I've got a picture," Ray added. He fished his phone from his pocket and handed it over. In one smooth movement, a lighter appeared in the man's hand and flashed open. A thin glow illuminated Amber's silhouette and seconds later a slight nod from the hooded man.

The sudden expulsion of air from one's lungs is both terrifying and shocking. Awareness of one's surroundings evaporates and is replaced by blinding pain. Pain that dropped Ray to his knees and left him helplessly gasping for breath.

"She's dead, old man."

"How do you know?" Ray managed to ask.

"Because I killed her."

"No." Ray saw the hooded one nod and a new level of pain spread across Ray's shoulders and exploded into the small of his back. Falling to his side, he was kicked and punched in the face, chest and stomach. After what seemed like an eternity, they stopped.

Ray groaned and blood bubbled from his nose. "Please," he blubbered. "Please," as if saying it twice would make a difference.

"Now. You're going back to Kansas," the hooded one responded. Pulling back his foot he pounded one last blow into Ray's groin. Then the lights snapped off.

———

Light slowly pulled at Ray and he opened his eyes. Never had his body felt like this. Not even when he caught amoebic dysentery on a mission trip to Nicaragua and heaved for three days.

No immediate idea of where he was or what had happened came to mind. No vowels or consonants formed into words in his mind.

Waves of unrealized pain rolled through his every nerve. Suddenly, he remembered.

Is she really dead? Or was he just trying to scare me?

Except for the city noises beyond it, the alleyway was still until it reverberated with the sound of a broken man retching. Ray spit bile and crawled to his knees, fighting as he struggled to regain equilibrium.

A bloody thread dangled from his chin like a spider's slivery strand. Dizziness gripped him as he tried to stand and the lights once again snapped off.

———

On the street, a plan can fragment in a matter of moments.

He blinked through swollen eyes and what felt like the worst sinus blockage he'd ever had. Would they beat him if they had nothing to protect? Maybe he was closer than he thought. Whatever the case, meeting Detective Mueller was unequivocally out of the picture. He couldn't be seen meeting with a cop now. Not that he could anyway. He wouldn't be going anywhere for a while. Reduced to a bloody mess, Ray felt every one of his fifty-four years.

Risking a hospital visit might prove fatal, he crept like a wounded animal back to his hotel room. He considered calling Carey to apologize, but wondered about phone taps. Maybe he'd watched too many TV shows.

Curled in the fetal position with hotel towels wrapped across his bloody scabs, he gulped several painkillers and begged for sleep.

His prayer answered, Ray slept heavy and woke sweating. He sat up, his head dizzy and pounding as he braced himself for a look in the mirror.

Black eyes, puffy cheeks, a rainbow of green, purple and yellow bruises, he resembled a pig in a butcher's window. The welts across his stomach and back were raw, open ruptures of red, but nothing prepared Ray for the agony between his legs.

I need to go to the hospital.

No. They'd be watching.

Desperate for a line to help him across the desolate expanse, Ray attempted to follow any thread of a plan he could find.

Anything. God show me. Tell me what to do.

The uncertainty built up through his addled mind and Ray suddenly felt sick again. Lunging for the toilet, he heaved again, though little came but intense, mind-numbing pain. Crawling, he tried to raise himself back into bed but instead, passed out again on the floor.

On day two, Ray awoke to someone pounding on his hotel door.

"Sir. Are you okay in there?"

Struggling to gain his composure, Ray peered through the peephole and saw the balding head of the hotel manager.

"Yes," he groaned. The pain persisted in his head. "Yes. I'm fine."

"Can you open the door Sir? Please?"

"I'm sorry." He looked down. What had he done with his clothes? "I'm not dressed."

"No worries, Sir. No worries," squeaked the manager. "Just checking. You paid for the week. I'll leave some new towels for you."

"Mmm. Thank you," Ray said rattling the deadbolt and then returned to the bed.

Dozing in and out for the next few hours, Ray finally awoke to a grumble from his empty stomach.

Good news, he thought as he limped to the shower.

"First food, then to see the detective," he said out loud. He still ached everywhere, but now that the worst seemed past, he no longer cared what they might do to him. And he knew they wouldn't jeopardize Amber's money-making potential. Though they might move her. He'd have to move fast. He'd already lost some good time.

"She needs me more than ever now."

Tears mixed with water from the shower, and Ray let them fall. They splashed down his cheeks, and rolled down his beaten body.

More than anything, Ray wished for all the pain to stop. It was time. For some reason, he remembered a slogan from a small business meeting he'd attended years ago. "Innovate or evaporate." Could he be stronger than his past and escape the tomb he'd accepted? The mental pain had taken its toll. And now physical pain had broken his stamina and threatened him with serious injury. But a new thought suddenly seized his brain and a warmth spread through his body.

It made sense. The man. What had he said?

"You're going back to Kansas."

He hadn't told anyone where he was from. Not even the convenience store guy.

They knew he was Amber's father.

She is *alive. And I'm close!*

Oh, thank you, Jesus.

Tears sprang to his eyes, but this time they were of joy.

"I'm close," he whispered. "Amber, I'm close."

He thought of Detective Mueller.

He needed his help.

But there was no doubt now: God was bringing everything he needed.

17

Smog-filtered light sliced through the half turned shades as Carey Mueller glanced across the sky view of his tenth floor window. Sighing with the boredom of it all he reached for a breath mint.

"Carey?" the assistant called through the intercom.

"Yeah."

"Your ten o'clock is on his way to you now."

"Okay. Thanks." Rummaging papers and quickly throwing a half-eaten bagel in the trash Carey wiped his mouth.

He really didn't have time for this.

"You owe me for this, Sheriff Murray T. Jackson," he muttered.

At the knock, he went to the door and opened it.

"Detective Mueller?" the man asked.

"That's me," Carey said.

"Ray Ellis."

"Take a seat, Ray," Carey said, backing up and indicating a chair across from the paper-strewn desk.

"Thanks. I appreciate your time. I'm sorry about canceling on you the other day."

Carey looked him over. "You okay?"

"Yeah, I think I will be."

"You get beat up?"

"I got the snot kicked out of me."

Ray shifted uncomfortably and Carey was silent. No man likes to admit defeat, he understood that. No need to rub salt in the wounds.

"Need anything? Coffee? Soda?" Carey offered.

"Coffee would be great."

Carey pressed a button, asked for two coffees and then looked squarely at Ray.

"I understand we have a mutual friend?"

"Sheriff Jackson is a good man."

"Said you had a story."

"Well, it's one I'm sure you've heard before. I know my daughter is just another unsolved missing child case. But . . ."

"For you it's not." Carey met Ray's tired eyes and saw a modicum of tension slide away.

Ray looked down again. "It's been a rough few days . . . I should never have left the café that day. Three guys in black jackets jumped me in the alley on 29rd Street. I woke up a couple days later wanting to scream. I'm angry, but honestly, I'm mostly just afraid. Of what I don't see, don't know. What I do know's bad enough. It's easier knowing she may be alive, but I tried all I could think of."

"Black jackets, you say? Big guys?"

Ray nodded.

Carey sat back, rubbing his chin. He wasn't prepared for this. Jackson made him expect a sad, desperate parent. And maybe Ray was that. But he'd evidently been successful enough to threaten someone, maybe Big George. "When you didn't show, I figured you went home.

"Well, I've thought about it plenty. Believe me. But truthfully I can't. Not until I know."

Carey took him in, considering. The guy would do anything. His eyes drifted to the picture of his four-year-old daughter Delaney. *So would you.* His pulse quickening, Carey turned his focus back on Ray.

Ray blinked back tears. "'She's gone, Ray,' they say. Everyone tells me there's nothing more that can be done. It's been six years." His voice choked with emotion. "I began to believe they might be right." Carey nodded, waiting, letting the silence steep between them.

"But deep down, I never believed that. I believe she's still out there. And I believe she needs me. But I'm not enough. I need help."

Carey watched as Ray's shoulders slowly began to quiver with stifled sobs.

Motion and time slowed as Carey's mind reached for the proper words. He'd consoled bereaved parents and calmed plenty of people. But never had he heard anything this impassioned before. Ever.

Slowly, he spoke. "All I can tell you is, you have to allow the pain. And let it hurt. Keep that edge. Don't fight it. Go with it. Can you do that?"

"I think so, Detective." Ray said with his head dangling toward the floor.

"Call me Carey. Figure we should use our real names if we're going to be friends."

Ray's head snapped up "Don't mess with me Carey. I need to know if you believe that Amber is still out there and not buried in a forgotten shallow grave by the river."

A mixture of emotions swept over Carey as the reality of this man's life splayed before him. He felt sorry for him. Pained. Angered. Just to name a few. Thoughts of Delaney and the earlier men's group battled in his mind.

Regaining his professionalism, Carey slowly fixed his gaze on Ray's broken face.

"Maybe they're right," he said. "Maybe it's over. Maybe you won't find Amber. But can I ask you something?"

A slight nod from Ray, so Carey proceeded.

"What do you really want from me?"

"Help me look for her. That's all."

The sudden piercing silence was filled with the thumping of their hearts. It demanded the truth, like a dirty secret, now exposed but unspoken.

Yesterday's prayer during his patrol burst fresh into Carey's mind bringing clarity to the action now crystalizing into focus.

A few days back, I wondered. What if you could save just one? Now it's looking me square in the eyes.

A few weeks ago, Carey would not have been prepared for this moment. He would have shaken it off with a chuckle and a handshake. But now he knew the danger of going all in with this guy and he held Ray's stare anyway.

He's the real deal, he heard in his mind. And something shifted inside him.

"If's she's alive, we're going to find her. I promise you."

Ray blinked, shocked. Carey rose from his desk and extended his hand toward Ray.

Ray took it. "Thank you." He held on with both hands, wincing against pain. "You have no idea how I've prayed for this day."

"That assault might be the best thing that could have happened. It gives us leads. Come on." He came around the desk. "First I'd like forensics to take a look at that eye."

Carey held open the door and Ray followed, grinning with pain.

———

Later that evening Ray crawled under the thin sheets of his Southside Chicago hotel room and laid his still throbbing head on the dank smelling pillow. Within moments he drifted into sleep.

What seemed only hours later, he awoke startled by the beeping of the hotel trash truck devouring its morning meal. Ray slowly let his mind wake. Lobe by lobe, from the cerebellum to the hippocampus his brain flickered to the events of the previous day with Detective Mueller. The events replayed before his eyes as he sorted through the encounter.

Suddenly he bolted upright.

No nightmare.

No cold sweat.

No screams.

Rolling over and staring at the peeling paint floating like popcorn hanging from the ceiling, it was there Ray realized the significance of this development. It was a miracle.

The nightmares had fled.

18

The corner of North and E streets swelled with people.

The First Baptist's free food every Saturday tended to do that.

Amber had seen it all before; church people would angelically appear in the red light district every Saturday morning to hand out clothes and food to the "poor and needy." Their love and concern for their fellow human beings was no more than a few drops in the bucket of a hopelessly dry desert.

But her stomach growled and Amber begrudgingly got in line. It moved quickly and soon Amber could see the tables. Little boxes of cereal stood piled up. Her favorite from when she was a girl caught her eye.

As she approached, she overheard two women whispering behind a portable wall.

"Every Saturday it's the same druggies and whores. Why do we bother?"

"Shh. They'll hear you."

"What? It's true. They won't change."

Amber peered through a crack in the wall. Two well-dressed, made-up women, sat in folding chairs, obviously there with the church.

Amber glared.

"Come on," the older brunette said, emerging from behind the partition. "Only an hour left. Then *shop-ping!*"

Something lurched inside and without thinking, Amber found herself walking up on them. "You two are so full of crap! How dare you judge what you don't understand. You hand out food so you can feel helpful and pretend you care. But you'd let us die just as soon as look at us."

Others had apparently overheard the women's conversation. Cheers and claps echoed from those standing in line.

A weather-beaten drunk who smelled like sewer added, "Yeah, get outta here!"

The stunned look on the women's faces showed they'd received a dose of shock therapy, and before she could stop it, someone was pressing Amber from behind as the shouts of angry protest rose louder.

"Get out of here!"

*"White trash *#%!"*

"Freaking soccer moms!"

"You want to judge me next?" a big black woman said. "Let's see you last one day out here, precious."

"You're no better than me, stuck-up, prissy-butts."

Soon, the church men nearby rushed to step in as the younger woman began to cry. "All right, everybody. Come on. Settle down."

Amber tore from the hallway and pushed her way back into the street. Her adrenaline pumping she wandered the concrete, fear pushing her along.

Why doesn't anyone really care?

Turning the corner, she saw "Teddy," one of her regular customers, looking out his car window from across the street. "Teddy"
had a driver and liked to take his girls uptown to his private place.
His eyes locked on Amber and she felt her heart sicken. The phrase
"they won't change," whispered through her mind. Was it true?
She didn't want this. The taste of it was sour and she only wanted
to vomit. Resting against the wall of the nearby cigarette store she
feigned exhaustion and avoided eye contact. After what seemed
longer than it was, the dark blue Mercedes with tinted windows
finally pulled away and meandered slowly into the stream of traffic on North Street. Amber continued standing against the wall,
attempting to blend in like a chameleon. She only wanted to be
left alone.

What did I just do? she thought. *What if he tells Big George?*

And she needed the money. This decision to go straight could
have grave consequences.

Turning Teddy down was a first step and it felt good but she
knew the road ahead would be treacherous. Still, it was a start.

Moments later, a taxi pulled up and stopped. Her heart quickened as she saw the two women from the food center. They were
oblivious, interested only in securing their taxi, and unaware of
Amber beneath the awning covering the store.

Crawling into the taxi they presumably were headed for the
suburban shopping malls. An uncontrolled urge passed through
Amber and like a marionette on a string, her hand dangled as if
reaching for the taxi. Desperation seized her and she imagined
running after them to beg them to take her with them. But she
stayed motionless, invisible. Slowly, she slid down the wall, the
rough stucco tearing at her shirt. The pain of realizing she'd been
reduced to this state was worse than the scraping of her back.

Exhausted and beaten, Amber pulled her keys from her purse and fumbled with the lock on her apartment door. She hadn't made any money for a while but Big George wouldn't send a collector until Tuesday. Somehow she would make it by then. She had made her mind up. A choice to change her life. A decision to sincerely follow Jesus Christ and his teachings. This was her new mission.

By some miracle, she'd already kicked the drugs. That was something that bore careful consideration. Not that she'd ever done them as much as some. But still, no withdrawals, no desire to even go back? She'd only ever heard of such a thing once in a testimony by someone at her old church back in Gilroy.

Funny. She hadn't thought of that in ages.

Stepping inside, she flicked on the light and glanced around. An orange-flowered couch with stains peered at her, as well as a coffee table littered with trash and dirty cups. The smell of stale ash, coffee, vodka, and cat litter filled the cramped atmosphere.

Home crap home, Amber fleetingly thought.

The incident at the mission still troubled her. Voicing her anger like that had frightened her. She hadn't known she really felt that way.

"Why are they always so quick to cast stones?" Her words bounced off the Chick-fil-A calendar that hung crookedly on her refrigerator.

As she crawled into bed, she laid her head on the pillow and stared at the ceiling. Weeks had passed since her last visit with Jesus and she reached on the floor and grabbed the Bible. Thumbing through the pages her eyes leapt from page to page until she saw the caption above chapter eight. "The woman caught in adultery."

Having grown up reading in the dark with a flashlight, she enjoyed continuing the tradition. She got her "itty bitty light" out and began to read.

The passage was only eleven verses so she read it three times, each time drawing her closer and closer like a force she couldn't escape.

The way the men longed to punish the woman, the response of Jesus, the parallels to her own life, it was all so familiar. Amber let the book slip from her grasp. Her eyes quietly closed.

She saw herself standing before Jesus in her best dress. Not yet asleep, she knew she wasn't quite dreaming, but it still had all the qualities of a nightmare. Instead of feeling bold and confident in his presence, this time she felt ashamed, like he could see right through her. She lay motionless, listening to the raspy sound of her breathing over the steady boom of her heart jumping out of her chest. What was real? It was a horrifying moment. A terrifying redefinition of herself that seeped into her heart and into the hollow place of her soul.

Suddenly she knew precisely, exactly, who she was. And in that moment between awake and asleep, she whispered to only herself what she now assuredly knew:

"This is the real me. I cannot deny it. I am that woman."

Curling into a ball, softly she slept.

———

It was a cool, crisp autumn morning and Amber knew instantly after reading the story what she had tried so vehemently to deny.

"I am who I am. This is the real me." At the precise moment of her personal epiphany Amber saw Jesus sitting on a stack of straw. Brown, yellow and light green, the forgotten strands formed a quilt across the ground. He waved and without a moment's hesitation she raced across the shimmering surface to him and said, "Those women deserved it you know. I was so spitting torqued. I wanted to rip them up. And then I wanted to escape with them!"

Looking at Jesus, Amber searched his face and eyes for understanding, for reassurance, for anything to justify her outburst.

Jesus did not answer for what seemed like forever. Instead his finger trailed on the ground and he began doodling in the dirt.

Amber quietly searched his face. It was as if he was restraining himself from comment while holding a softness in his eyes that exuded deep love. Confused, Amber held her tongue and waited.

"I know Amber. I was there," Jesus softly spoke. He continued drawing quietly in the soft earth.

Silence hung like a dark veil between them until Amber finally spoke, "Tell me about the woman caught in adultery."

"They wanted to stone her. But they were looking for a way to get me," Jesus began. "Remember verse six from chapter eight?"

Amber's eyes scrunched and she eased back onto a loose pile of yellow straw. Glancing at the slow moving clouds she slowly nodded no.

Jesus began quoting, "*They were using the question as a trap, in order to have a basis for accusing him. Our law commands us to stone such a women. What do you say?*"

Amber's gaze shifted to the eastern horizon. "They were judging her."

"Back then, the big sins were idolatry, murder and adultery. I told them to stop judging by appearances. They thought the external was what made people righteous. But you know—I look at the heart."

"But why is it always about the woman?" The words gushed from Amber. "What happened to the man? Was he allowed to go free?"

124

Jesus's eyes filled with tenderness. "Women have always been mistreated by powerful men. This was a set-up from the start. She was a pawn in their game, their sacrificial lamb. Some of them wanted her and this was the expression of their jealousy."

"I know the feeling," Amber softly said.

"As a known prostitute, someone paid to spend the night with her. And at the pre-arranged moment the trap was sprung. They burst in and the woman was dragged out like a criminal. The man was allowed to disappear." Jesus breathed quickly. "It was a tricky situation."

Pausing as if reliving the moment, he continued, "If I agreed to stone her, I'm not who I said. And if I say to let her go, I'm guilty of breaking Moses' law."

Crumbled earth sifted through his fingers. Arrested by the movement Amber asked. "Is that when you began drawing in the dirt?"

"It was too much for me to bear. I felt shame and sadness for that woman."

"What did you write?"

"Does it matter?" Jesus softly spoke.

"I want to know," Amber pressed.

"How do you know I wrote something? Maybe I drew a picture. I'm a pretty good artist, you know."

"What did you draw then?" Amber casually responded.

Jesus smiled, letting his eyes take Amber in.

"Words like treachery, lust, hypocrisy. Things like that."

"They knew you meant them."

Jesus slowly nodded. "'If any of you is without sin, let him be the first to throw a stone at her.'"

Amber watched him. "It was like you said, "Yes. Go ahead. But be prepared to have your skulls cracked, too, because you're as guilty as her."

A slight chuckle emitted from Jesus.

"And then you said, 'Where are they?' 'Cuz they were gone, right?"

"Yes. But remember I asked her a second question."

"Oh. I don't remember that. What was it?" Amber puzzlingly replied.

"'Has no one condemned you?'"

"I didn't come to change the law. I came to redefine it. All of us need forgiveness. So I gladly offered it."

"But had she asked for it? Did she believe?"

"Well, she gave the answer of the forgiven," Jesus paused.

"'No one, sir,'" Amber echoed.

"Everyone is a sinner. No better or worse than a prostitute in need of forgiveness."

Amber shifted as the straw slowly slipped her sideways. "If she'd tried justifying herself or blaming others . . . would that have changed your answer?"

"Yes. It's hard to see what you're being offered when you're complaining about what you don't have. But she did none of that. She basically said, 'I'm guilty as charged.' But forget all that. All that matters right here, right now, is you and me. So let me ask you a question."

He locked eyes with her, and sliding with his knees across the shimmering surface of yellow stalks he took her face in his hands. Without flinching she laid her hands over his and inhaled. "Amber, my sweet daughter. Where are your accusers?"

The air rushed from her lungs. Her breakdown was instantaneous and complete. No pretense, nothing held back, just the tears of many years held over long, anguished days and nights. The silent hurt finally relented and released. All the misunderstanding, the mountains of shame, the acres of anguish and pain were wrapped into the words.

Huge sobs escaped her and she slumped face down to the ground as tears fell to the soft earth. Amber's black hair covered her face, but Jesus reached out his hand and placed it on her head. "'Go now, and sin no more.'"

———

Awaking from her sleep, Amber rose and went to take a lukewarm shower.

What did the woman do after she encountered Jesus? How did she get out?

She stood in the water and allowed it to cascade over her head. Closing her eyes, she prayed. "Help me, Jesus. Help me!"

Just like when you stopped using, I will be here. Trust Me.

Flipping off the nozzle, she stood there. Like cold air seeping through a plastic sheet, the thought flickered into her head.

He'd help me. If I'd only let him.

"Awesome," Amber exclaimed as she dried off. "I'm talking to myself again."

Moments later, she bumbled around the kitchen scrounging for food. "Please let there be coffee!" she shouted as she pulled open the canister. Popping the lid, she rejoiced. But it triggered the same thought as before.

Could she simply stop ignoring her pain?

She made coffee and plunked down with her steaming cup on the couch, the only furniture in her tiny apartment. She spied a scrap of paper beneath a stained Glamour magazine and pulled it out.

Call me if you need anything. —Rachel

Inspiration struck as squarely as if she'd whacked her head on the cabinet door. This was her chance. Tossing aside all pretense, she picked up her phone, breathed deep and dialed the number.

On the way to the coffee shop, she fought feeling nervous and embarrassed. She had no money. And what if her stomach growled the whole time?

She couldn't worry about that now. Jesus was all over this.

The Kansas Jayhawks scarf had been a dead giveaway—when Amber admitted she didn't remember what Rachel looked like, Rachel said she'd be wearing a Jayhawks scarf.

It had been Amber's dad's favorite team. "I think I hear you, Jesus. I really do."

As she arrived, Amber spotted her immediately and slid into the booth. Rachel's smile was as genuine as she remembered. The scarf stirred memories of better days within her, the television up loud and her dad cheering from his old recliner. She fought back the emotion.

"Hi," Rachel said, offering her hand.

"Thank you for meeting me Amber."

"It's so nice to meet you."

Hearing her name used brought chills, and somehow a warmth deep in her bones.

"Is everything okay?"

"I'm just—it's strange using my real name." Struggling for composure Amber stumbled out the words she hadn't uttered in a long time. "My friend, Kena, was the last to call me that." Wiping the side of her face with the back of her hand, Amber quickly dug in her purse for a Kleenex.

"Here. I got an extra," Rachel said, handing it over.

"Thanks," Amber mumbled. "I seem to be a fountain these days. I love the scarf, by the way. Did you go to KU?"

"Yeah. But just one year."

"Oh."

Dropping her head, Rachel gave a small sniffle. "I—I think I'm over it. But maybe I'm not."

Amber nodded, waiting for explanation.

"His name was Jared," Rachel said. "He promised me the moon. And stars." Pausing, she sniffed and took out another tissue. "But that's that. I made my own bad choices. Drugs. Prostitution. All of it. Suffice it to say, I know your situation. But can I help you? Trust me, I'm a good listener."

Amber smiled. "Why are you doing this?"

"Because I have to," replied Rachel. "I was rescued. I'm playing the religion card, but hear me out. Jesus Christ made a difference in my life. Well, and—" she stopped to wipe her eyes. "my friend who helped me kick the drugs and alcohol."

The human psyche's capacity for misery is immense. Daily abuse, neglect, and loss build and exact a toll. Loaded with megatons of hurt and resentment, Amber was a reservoir at extreme flood level. Would Rachel be the warrior of strength she needed?

Sensing her sincerity and the Holy Spirit, she decided to trust her and Amber poured out the last six years of her life.

Two caramel macchiato's later, Amber asked Rachel. "How do you go on? I mean how do you keep pretending you're fine when deep down you know you're a rotten mess?"

"One time," Rachel began, "back at KU, a bunch of my girlfriends and I went out to this bar and ended up meeting this 'prince,' or so he claimed. Some dinky country in the Middle East. But he was cute and we were goofy. Everyone had a couple drinks and we starting talking about sex. Who knows why but all the girls were flirting with him. Crazy. And he said some disgusting things. And I remember thinking, he's degrading every girl in this room. We're just toys to this guy. He's totally using us."

SEPULCHRE

Rachel continued, "Sadly, I sat there grinning like a fool. I kept listening and pretending, and I wanted to punch him in the mouth."

"Of course," Amber nodded.

"You stay because you don't know how to escape," Rachel said.

Later, Amber would reflect how strange it was that the same words could be exchanged between people and mean nothing. But at the right time, a whole different meaning could arise in a single flare, and that sentence could forever alter a person's life.

You stay because you don't know how to escape.

Amber turned away and gazed out the window. In that moment, it defeated, rather than comforted her. The conviction of it was too strong.

"I've met women like you for a while now. Similar situation, the same body language, turning away, trembling fingers. They all want out of prostitution. But they wonder how. They know they'll be unwelcome by society. Tainted creatures. Branded troublemakers. Right?" Rachel pointed. "The reflection in that window was a mirror image of myself less than 5 years ago."

Something floated in the space between them as the seconds passed, something fleeting like sparks across the sky. Finally Amber lifted her eyes to meet Rachel's.

"Are you guilty of everything you imagine you've done?"

"What—snorting drugs? Swilling alcohol? Sex with strangers for money?"

"Yeah, all that."

Amber nodded. "But," and dropping her chin, Amber sighed. "I'm done with all that. For good."

Rachel smiled. "I believe you. And I'm so proud of you."

The words streaked to Amber's heart and streamed across her face, raising her head with hope.

Not a single living soul had listened or believed a word she'd said in the last six years. But Rachel understood. She saw her.

Staring deeply at her, Amber probed. "Rachel?"

"Yes, Amber?"

With broken breaths and heavy heart, she asked the only thing she wanted to know. "Can I trust you?

Without hesitation Rachel responded. "Of course, hon."

Amber pleaded. "Help me escape?"

Laying her hand softly on Amber's open palm, Rachel said, "How do you want to start?"

"First, I need to get brave. I may need a job."

"Good. One step at a time." Rachel smiled. "First. Let's pray. And then let's talk about what you love."

19

Leaning in the cramped hotel shower, Ray prayed for what must have been the thousandth time since beginning this terrifying adventure. He needed answers, patience, bravery, anything to give him and ultimately his daughter hope.

Suddenly, like lightning flashing across his mind, inspiration struck and an idea followed like the corresponding crash of thunder.

During his research about the sex trade in Chicago, he'd read a story of a mother searching for her daughter who ran to the city and was caught in a web of sex, drugs and alcohol. Undeterred, the mother went looking for her prodigal. She wouldn't accept that her daughter was lost in the sea of humanity, and she simply placed pictures of her anywhere she might be seen. Each was inscribed with a simple note. "I love you, Corrine. Please come home."

It had worked. Somehow, they'd reunited and her daughter went home.

He hadn't remembered it until now, but the story burned inside him. He turned off the water and grabbed a towel. He didn't want to wait, didn't know if he could. But he couldn't do this alone, regardless of what miracles others had experienced. He couldn't endanger the mission. He'd never succeed without Carey's know-how.

He wrapped the towel around him and paced the small room like a caged animal. The search would be on soon enough. And he'd just wait until then. He could do it. He had to.

An impossibly long 14 minutes passed and his phone finally beeped.

I'm here.

Grabbing a banana and a granola bar, he forced himself to walk to the curb where Carey waited in his car.

"How'd you sleep?"

"Not bad. Didn't move much."

"I bet. That was some beating you took." He pointed to the two cups in the console. "You need coffee. Auntie Chin across the street makes a good cup."

"Thanks."

"So, game plan."

"Yeah." Ray took a sip.

"First, you gotta know something." Carey grabbed his own cup. "We don't always find what we're looking for. And even when we do, the pain doesn't necessarily go away."

"You sound like my pastor," Ray said.

Carey laughed. "Maybe mine is rubbing off on me."

Ray suddenly felt warmer. He knew there was something special about this guy. But he hadn't wanted to presume. And he didn't want to cross professional lines now. He'd follow Carey's lead. But he nodded and smiled. "I had a feeling you had a deeper motive here."

"Definitely," Carey said. "But listen, you gotta know when to cover the holes in your heart. Remember. It's not a race. It's a journey."

Ray nodded. "I understand." He wanted to tell Carey about the conflict in his mind. Tell it and let it gush like a broken pipe. But he kept the words held, exhaled deeply and said, "Wise words. I hear you, I really do. I'm just so grateful."

Carey sniffed and pulled out a folder. "Me too. I'd nearly given up. If you hadn't shown up, I just might have."

Ray considered him and said nothing. But in that moment, he knew his defenses were down. "Someone once told me if you stop feeding the pain it will dissipate. Not necessarily go away. 'Cause it may never fully go away."

Carey paused flipping pages and looked up. "Sometimes you think it's gone. And then suddenly your heart is squirming like a trapped animal in your chest."

Ray felt the animal in his own chest realizing he was possibly getting more than he'd bargained for from this virtual stranger. But he willed himself not to look away.

Note to self, he thought. *More to come.*

A quiet fog settled over them and Ray imagined each was remembering the dreams they'd had and the losses they'd experienced. They could lie dormant for years, but spring up so unexpectedly and press into daily existence in a moment. Who could tell the difference between hope and despair? Each wore such clever disguises.

Pulling away from the curb, Carey slid the clipboard between the seats. "So. The plan?"

"Yes, the plan."

Carey looked over his shoulder and merged into traffic. "Assuming she's a walker now, she's watched. Doesn't mean we can't pose as Johns and find her, but we also can't just go stupid and start asking around. We have to keep a low profile. If she's Big George's, not even cops are safe."

"What?" Ray sounded incredulous. "How is that even possible?"

Carey sighed. "He's been ignored too long. Like the old mafia, he's gotten too powerful, too well-protected. The money flows in and he knows how to spend it."

Ray listened, trying to take it in. There was a real possibility this may get them both killed. What was Carey's end game?

"Still," Carey said, "I'm reasonably assured—and I told my captain as much—Big George isn't about to kill anyone in broad daylight and risk his entire business. So we ask around during the daytime."

Ray agreed. "Sounds good."

"We'll put the precinct number on the flyers and we can ask businesses in the neighborhood to post them. We just can't let them see you—you're a target now." Carey cracked his neck. "And I'll be disguised too." He pointed to a sack in the back seat. "With any luck, we'll just look like a couple of concert promoters and we'll have a couple days to see what we find before they notice anything."

"You think this will work?"

"It isn't likely Amber will see one. But we might get lucky. And who knows? We might kick over the whole rat's nest and see them scatter."

Ray grinned. "Oh yeah. Me wanna play whack-a-mole."

Carey laughed. "I like you, Ray. You are one funny dude."

Ray put his arm on Carey's shoulder. "We'll be careful. Where to first?"

The next day, Carey asked the elderly couple that ran the neighborhood convenience shop if they'd seen the girl in the picture. They hadn't. The search had intensified after yesterday. Bars, hotels, nightclubs, any place a walker might frequent, they visited them all in their blue rock band jackets, ball caps and beards. Soon one day became two, and the urgency was palpable. A life was at stake. Every second counted. But as the day wore on, Carey knew he'd soon have to face his commanding officer. He had taken personal time, with a "divisional provision." Just two days, the captain had said. He was sympathetic, but he'd spoken with the captain that morning.

You've done what you can, Mueller. Time's up. I've got a division to run. I want these pieces of trash as bad as you do.

Maybe, maybe not, Carey had thought. But they'd already hit all the places Amber might go if she was here. They'd talked briefly with people on the streets and shops and they were about out of places and pictures of Amber anyway. Ray had included a simple note on the bottom of each picture. "Amber-lamb. Nothing else matters. I love you. Please call. —Daddy." No one cared what they were posting. And using his office number ensured there was no way anyone could trace it to Ray.

And yet, for the first time in his Christian life, Carey honestly felt peace in his spirit. A peace that Christ had whispered to him the night before through the Bible as he read.

I'm leaving you peace. I'm giving you my own peace. I don't give gifts in the way the world does. Don't let your heart be troubled; don't be fearful.

Carey glanced across the room at Ray standing silently before the cluttered bulletin board. Scraps of paper promoting events, people and places, they overwhelmed the simple photo. Carey moved to join him.

"God, let Amber find this and know she is loved," Ray said. "And let her pimp expose himself so I can throw his butt in jail." Ray turned around. "Amen."

"Amen," echoed Carey.

"Where to next?" Ray pressed.

Carey smiled, pitying him. Both knew their time was about up. "Just one section on the south edge we haven't covered yet."

Ray nodded. "Let's do it."

———

Zedd slid his phone from his pocket and held it up. Slipping behind the streetlight, he began clicking pictures of Carey and Ray.

"What are these crazy freaks doing?" He watched them go into another shop down the crowded street.

Time to find out.

Pulling his hoodie up, he strolled into the shop recently vacated by the two men.

Questioning the shop keeper could give him away. But he persisted. "What'd those guys want?"

"Nothing. Couldn't help them," the big man said.

Zedd scoffed and exited. He trailed the men, stopped short, seeing the shorter man peering through the dirty windows of Sid's Brews then watched as he taped a picture in the corner.

Zedd stayed back from the window and backed into the alley.

Misty. Bingo.

Watching the men exit, Zedd waited. He silently stepped inside Sid's and snatched the photo from the window. He left, walking the other way, stuffing the photo into his pocket. He pulled out his phone and dialed.

20

"This is what I want!" Big George exclaimed and extended his fist for a quick knuckle bump from Zedd. "This is how you get things done," he roared.

"Everybody, over here. It's time to solve a problem."

"He's putting these up!" Big George held up the flyer Zedd had brought, and George smashed his massive fist on the table. The sound echoed like a bomb exploding in the empty warehouse.

Dirt particles flashed into the glow of low-hanging incandescent lights. Filthy on both the inside and out, the warehouse was a forgotten parlor of pain and suffering for Big George's operations.

"Listen up, jackwads. Somebody better tell me Misty isn't going to see these. I'm gonna bust somebody up."

Zedd was the only one who looked calm, fingering the jagged scar that ran from his cheek to his chin. The room stilled and the tension settled like ash.

His massive thighs surging beneath the folding table Big George pulled a black Beretta 9-millimeter from his jacket and pointed it at a neon sign hanging on the wall. Destitute, empty and abandoned, Zedd doubted a gun emptied into a target of mortar or flesh would gather a single notice. Gazing down the sight as if eyeing prey, Big George clicked his tongue and said "Boom."

Nothing was tiny about George Mitchell Stevens. Raised by a single mother who worked two jobs in South Chicago, by age fifteen he'd been arrested seven times. By age eighteen, his mother had kicked him out and his "antics," as his mother called them, included sex trafficking, drugs and suspected murder.

And nothing had changed about him for over 20 years but his weight and his hairline.

Early on, someone had tried to reverse label him "Tiny" but he'd disappeared. Ever since, he'd been Big George. At 310 pounds and five feet ten, the name stuck.

While other pimps ran modern outfits, George fashioned himself an "old school" don. He demanded respect, plain and simple. He'd seen *The Godfather* movies and didn't care much if people "got" him. He was satisfied when he got what he wanted, when he was respected.

He'd risen to prominence using fear and his ruthless logic. And he'd always been his own biggest hero, providing a valuable service to the community he served.

"Does she know yet?" he bellowed. No one responded. Nobody knew for sure where Misty was or why she'd always been one of Big George's favorites. Zedd suspected her toughness and attitude reminded George of his youngest sister who was killed as a teenager with a random bullet from a street shooting.

"She'd better not. I've provided my girl everything—food, shelter and security. And she's my best entertainer."

Someone spoke up. "Not Candy?" He looked around for approval. "She's pretty sweet."

It was the newbie. Like a giant cat leaping for its meal, Big George was instantly upon him. A swift backhand knocked the kid down and George pounded on him as the men cringed.

"Get him out of my sight!" George screamed, looking like a crazed animal.

Unceremoniously, two men dragged the unconscious victim across the room and deposited him among the crates and empty boxes.

George Stevens also understood intimidation. It was survival instinct, but it pleased him to thrash anyone. His will was not easily dismissed. It had won him the Southside.

"Anyone else want to question my business?" George hissed, staring each of them down. Big George scanned the faces unwilling to meet his stony glare. Satisfied, George grinned and sat, announcing to the room, "The first round is on me tonight, boys."

Mumbles of appreciation punctuated the silence and Big George held up his hand. "But. I got a job for you."

One asked through chipped teeth, "We get to have some fun?" He smiled expectantly.

"Oh yeah," cooed Big George. "Big fun!"

The plan was relatively simple, like "shooting zombies at the arcade." The smaller guys would find Misty, keep her occupied while they could remove the flyers, and the others would find the detective and the old man, and force them into a designated dead-end alley.

"Bullets to the head. Nobody will know a thing. Zip and Junior, get it done and then lay low." Big George would call when he thought the heat was off and each would receive a nice bonus for "killing it like pros," as he called it.

"And I don't want any bleeders," he added with a cocked fist. "No games. We take Mueller and old dude out. Nice and quiet in the alley. Got it?"

Zedd spoke carefully. "Boss? Mueller? That'll bring the heat."

"I don't care! He knows what's he's into. And he'll get what's coming. I'm Big George. I can't tolerate any messing with my business. Mueller has cost me three girls already with his Mother Teresa act. No more! He goes down. Besides, I'm smarter. I want it to rain bullets on that stupid Five-O."

"But first, I make him an offer he can't refuse," he mimicked, giving his best imitation of Marlon Brando.

Big George's eyes darkened, the wheels turning in his giant head.

"What you thinking, Boss?" Zedd asked.

"The old man. I think I'll do the honors myself." He punctuated each word as if seeing it play out in his head. "It's time people remember who they're dealing with. This ends here. It's time I got back in the game." George made a slashing motion across his throat.

The obedient soldiers each nodded. And Big George sneered.

21

"Hi, Amber."

Clouds floated across the sky of various shapes and sizes. Suddenly, his familiar face appeared.

"Jesus. You surprised me. I was just reading." And holding up the black book, she waved it slightly. "I'm so glad you came. Would you mind telling me about the disabled man you healed at the pool of . . . Beth something?"

"Bethesda." Jesus chuckled. "Great choice." He pulled off his ball cap and wiped his brow.

Amber noticed the moisture, and the sudden realization that he may be sweating surprised her.

I never thought of him being so . . . human, she mused.

"Can we move to the shade?" he said pointing to the tree at the edge of the field.

"Sure." Amber led and Jesus followed, taking big steps in his boots.

"You read the story?" Jesus asked as they walked through the short green shoots of corn sprouting in perfectly laid rows.

"Well, yeah. I mean I read it, but I wanted it from your perspective."

They settled beneath the rustling green leaves of the old pecan tree.

"This is nice. Thank you," Jesus murmured as he slowly slid to sit at the base of the tree. "I guess that's the trick, right?" Jesus said, his voice trailing off. "Getting my perspective."

The silence was long and deep. Amber waited, watching him. His head remained motionless, but his hidden dark brown eyes darted like fireflies beneath his closed eyelids as if the images were being replayed there.

"The hopelessness that emanated from that place. The Pool of Bethesda was a huge place with a lot of helpless, superstitious people. So many people fighting for space, fighting to believe in the magic. It was more than I could stomach," Jesus quietly spoke.

The tone of his voice made her catch her breath. The depth of his contemplation told her he was reliving the moment.

"He was known as an invalid. And he believed it. Just hoping for the waters to move. They believed that you know? Beneath the pool was a subterranean stream, which now and then would bubble up and disturb the water. They said an angel caused it and the first person to get into the pool would be healed."

Jesus stared straight ahead over the field. "I remember thinking, what unbearable desperation brings people here? What depth of ignorance causes a man to lie here for 38 years, wasting his life? Thirteen-thousand, eight-hundred and seventy days of ignorance that slowly devolved into excuses and despair. When I saw him lying there I could only think of one question."

"'Do you want to get well?'" Amber said. "Kind of a weird question."

"Maybe. Maybe you're right. But I wanted to hear him say it. He had to believe I could help him. The greatest obstacle to healing isn't lack of faith. It's their lack of desire to be healed."

"But you healed him anyway. I don't understand . . ." her voice tapering off. Amber thought of her own situation. *Did she really want to be well?*

"He wasn't even close enough to get in the pool if it did stir. He allowed himself to be pushed aside. His hope had died there. But he hadn't considered what else he could do."

Finally opening his eyes, Jesus stared at Amber and spoke in a measured tone. "A lot of people are like that man. You know what I mean?"

Scarcely breathing, Amber dipped her head.

"They've given up being responsible for themselves, given up being whole, they keep crawling back to their familiar spot telling themselves they're invalid when they're just being disobedient."

Amber began to tremble, willing herself not to cry. Jesus placed a hand on her arm and she immediately calmed down. He was so kind and yet . . . so right.

"They're afraid, and they won't believe the truth that they can be free through the truth they've been shown. In fact, they fear getting well."

Amber looked up into his eyes. "Because if they actually were healed, then what would they do?"

Jesus nodded slowly. "And they could claim that self-pity as their identity for years and turn into shells of who they really are."

Amber felt tears slipping from her eyes. Suddenly Jesus held up his hand and pinched his fingers together. "They're this far away from it, just enough to claim it isn't their fault. And nobody knows the truth but them and God."

Amber's heart felt like it would beat out of her chest. Jesus stood and began to pace. His scuffed cowboy boots pressed into the soft earth. Dusting his hands off on his jeans, he leaned against the tree and looked down at her. "Often what we do and what we think we want are two very different things. So let me ask you, Amber . . ."

Amber closed her wet eyes against what she knew he would ask.

"Do you really want to be well?"

Swallowing, Amber felt all the blood in her body drain to her toes.

"I do, Jesus. I mean, seeing you and knowing you now, here, I really do."

"Stopping the drugs and the sex doesn't erase the pain of the shame. What will you do with that?"

"I don't know. I mean, I just think I'm so totally helpless. I can't get free on my own." Amber felt the words escape and immediately eased from having said them.

"That's too easy. That's what he said. No one can help."

The stark truth landed on her and in her desperation, Amber thought, *Maybe I could still help myself, if I only had a gun.*

If only my knight in shining armor would arrive.

If only safety existed somewhere in this broken world.

If only . . .

"How can I help myself? How can I ever get free without your help? We all want God's help, but he doesn't come!"

Tears slid down Amber's face, but she stumbled on. "I want to get well. And I need you. But . . ." Catching her breath, she stopped.

"Go on," Jesus said, his voice soft and soothing.

"I just have to believe you have always been here." She looked up.

Jesus smiled. "Faith is a gift given by God. Your power is his power. Throw in love and you've got all the ingredients you need." Jesus' voice softened to a whisper. "That's grace in action."

Kneeling, Jesus stretched out his hand toward her sitting cross-legged. "What do you say, Amber?"

146

The tension released and she grasped his hand and fell forward onto her face in dirt. "Oh, Jesus. I need you. Please help me." Her breath came in shallow gasps. "I need you to take it all. All my shame—All the dirty things I've done. Oh, Jesus, please. Take all of me."

Taking her in his arms, Amber slowly pulled herself up to him. He held her, tight around her shaking shoulders.

After several moments, she looked him in the eyes.

"I am so sorry."

"It was forgiven long ago, my sweet daughter."

She nodded. "I know. But I'll always need your healing."

"Not always. Not in the same way." He brushed her hair from her face. "You are free of all that now. You will not walk in the way you did ever again. Today you are healed, my child."

22

The damp fall air hung as Amber stepped from her apartment building and into the street. Sunlight drizzled through the buildings turning the sky grayish blue. The air caressed her face and she wondered whether her jean shorts and tank were enough for the day. *I don't have to be freezing all day anymore. I'm getting out of here. But how? That was the real question.*

Rachel had warned her of the peril. "It won't be easy. It won't be simple. You have to be smart. They will be watching you."

For a girl who had never liked the cold, the past months hadn't been easy. The breeze picked up and she turned to head back in and grab a sweatshirt.

"Hey, sexy!"

"Want some good stuff?"

Whistles and catcalls serenaded her from the nearby corner. The "Ridgetop Butchers," they patrolled the streets, selling drugs and other things. She knew them all.

"You boys can't afford me. Forget it."

"Doesn't cost anything to look," quipped Wolf, the acknowledged leader.

"Take your stuff and shove it," she yelled reentering the door and bolted up the stairs.

It never ends, she thought. *All my life I've been a piece of meat to everybody.* Pausing inside her door, she caught her breath. It was almost Tuesday and Big George's man would be coming. Yet strangely she was at peace. She had absolutely no idea where the money was coming from. What could she do? Fight harder, stop caring, run faster, be stronger?

Seek Jesus, she thought. *That's all you need now.*

"Better hurry, you're late," she thought. *"Late. Late for what? Or not late enough? Hmm? I'll have to think about that one."* Either way she had no clue what to do with herself.

Snatching a look in the mirror, she went to her closet and quickly found the right jacket and reset her outfit in the dust-streaked glass. A sudden clarity flashed into her mind, and for the first time a new shard of truth struck her.

Yes, she was a hooker. Yes, she'd slept with strangers for money. But she was different now for what she knew. What she'd now heard. A different song. And it had changed her and it rang strangely familiar even now and warmed her ears as she hummed the tune.

"Jesus loves me," she whispered. "This I know."

She was forgiven. And for the first time in forever, she knew that. For now, it was all that mattered, the only significant point tethering her to life.

She'd been claimed from the sepulcher of death.

She blinked and yawned. Hard. *Caffeine.* Before she thought of what to do next, she needed coffee.

"Yes, me need strong drink," she said to the air, recalling the goofy way her father had joked. She grabbed her key and headed downstairs, out the door, and up the street to Auntie Chin's small cafe a few blocks north.

Three blocks later, Amber casually stopped and pulled a small mirror from her purse. Appearing to check her makeup she tilted the mirror in order to glance backwards. Sure enough, one of the Ridgetop Butchers was standing about half a block behind her. *"So they are watching me!"* she hastily thought. *"What now?"*

The smell of fresh bread and coffee filled Amber's nostrils. Auntie Chin's was warm and welcoming, and Amber drank it in, the smells, the kindness, and the freedom. A freedom she didn't have many places; to enjoy a hot cup of coffee and a warm roll. The freedom to sit and be a normal person. "Normal"—whatever that could mean for her.

She quickly reminded herself she had a taker for that kind of shame now.

"How you today, child?" Auntie Chin asked peering over the counter. Auntie Chin was short but made up for it with big personality and a feisty temper. Even the thugs of the neighborhood left her alone.

Could she trust her?

"I'm fine, Auntie Chin. How are you?"

"Good, child. I good."

Amber bit back emotion, and quickly turned to wander the quaint little shop filled with trinkets, toys, and delicacies from across the Pacific.

Pausing in the crowded aisles she allowed her mind to wander to the world that existed across the ocean. Filled with people and places so unknown to her. So distant. So surreal. Drinking in the atmosphere, she escaped momentarily to new surroundings and dreamed of another life. Her imagination flashed and the sensations were inviting.

What if I just got on a plane and went to China? Told them all to go screw themselves? Amber thought looking at a picture on a postcard of the Great Wall of China.

There's more than one wall to that idea, she reflected. But the thought gave her solace.

"You want a coffee?"

"I'm sorry, not today. I'm a little short on cash."

"No. I mean for free."

"Really?"

"Sure. I like you. You seem sad."

"Oh no! Actually I'm happy. Very happy. Something wonderful has happened."

"You tell me. Okay?"

"I like happy!"

Swallowing hard she eased the words from her throat. "I'm clean. For the first time in six years. I'm off the drugs."

"That good. I clean too."

Without a sound Auntie Chin rolled up her sleeve and flashed a track marked arm.

"Twenty years. Never go back."

"Wow!" gushed Amber. "Wow."

"You kick hard?" Auntie Chin remarked.

"I just decided one night. And in the morning I was fine. It was weird."

"Not weird. Faith. You say. In action."

Amber stilled as the sudden exposure of her guts lay hanging all over the floor.

"I better go. I'm sorry. I'm late."

"Take sweet roll too, please."

"Oh. Thanks."

"You come back soon. Talk anytime."

Looking around the store, she sighed. The fog in her head seemed to be dissipating and feeling energized by the drink and food she headed for the door.

Strange how you can walk by something a hundred times and never really see it. Amber had walked out of Auntie Chin's a hundred times and never noticed the bulletin board. But today, a fluttering picture jumped off the board at her. Someone was looking for a girl who looked familiar, about her age. Her lips moved reading over the words, "Amber-Lamb, please come home." She said it again, the caption not registering.

"It doesn't matter. I love you. Please call me - Daddy."

In a flurry, Amber re-read it. And again. The caption. The name. *What in the world? Someone had the same nickname she used to?*

Amber felt the coffee burning in her hand and glancing down noticed the shake in her wrist. Her breath came short. She set the cup on the nearest table and grabbed the picture from the board.

"Do you know who put this picture up?"

Auntie Chin pulled her glasses up from the chain around her neck.

"Sorry. I blind these days." She gazed at the picture then at Amber, then to the picture.

Lowering her glasses slowly, she said, "I don't know who put this up. But I know who this girl is."

She paused for a moment that seemed to stretch into eternity.

"It you."

Amber stared.

"Go look in mirror, girl. It you. Someone looking for you."

The words dawned on Amber like a light through fog.

"For me?" she mumbled.

Auntie Chin grinned, nodding vigorously.

"I—I need to use the restroom."

"Here. Take key."

Amber grabbed the giant plastic spoon and walked on shaky legs downstairs. The mirror on the wall was scratched and grimy, but Amber could see clearly. Holding up the photo, she looked at her face and then at it. The girl had black hair. Amber was blonde. But her hair was once black. The eyes, nose, cheeks, they resembled her.

It couldn't be. It was too unlikely. But how could there be another Amber-lamb who looked like her? Her legs threatened to give out and she grasped the sink.

Could it be?

Daddy? She stared into her eyes and watched the tears form.

Either way, the odds seemed too great for it not to be him.

Stuffing the photo in her coat, she dabbed her eyes to erase the tear stained smudges. Breathing shallow, she climbed the stairs and dropped the key on the counter, leaving without saying anything. She pushed into the street and allowed it to swallow her.

23

The Lake Michigan clouds hung fat and dark as they settled over the concrete jungle of South Chicago. It was an inky black night even as the streets buzzed with electricity. Carey glanced at his watch as he and Ray walked out of the China Palace following a quick, but late supper.

"Eating after 11:30 pm and all that fried food!" Pausing, Carey groaned. "I'm gonna pay for this Ray."

Ray laughed. "Me too." He rubbed his belly. "But it sure was good. Thanks for—"

Shoomp!

Most people can only speculate about the sound of a bullet whizzing past and exploding into buildings. But it wasn't the first time Detective Mueller had heard it.

Instantly he knew the shot was meant for him. A loud *smack* punctuated the noise of traffic on E Street and caused panic in several bystanders who immediately screamed and ran.

On instinct, Carey ducked and grabbed his gun. Ray heard the small explosion before he saw the shavings crumbling from the brick wall behind Carey's head.

"Get down, Ray!" he heard himself shouting.

"What was that?"

"Someone's shooting at us."

Smack!

Smack!

"Stay down!" Carey said. "And follow me."

"Carey?"

"Trust me, Ray. Do exactly what I tell you and we'll live to see tomorrow."

Ray nodded.

"When I say go, get up and run as fast as you can to that alley." He pointed to the alley about thirty yards in front of them. "And stay behind me! Got it?"

Glass shattered and the front window of the China Palace restaurant rained down in tiny shards onto their heads.

"Now, Ray. Now!"

And suddenly Carey was up and moving. Ray saw Carey's gun waving slightly in the air and heard the *thunk . . . thunk . . . thunk . . .* of his weapon.

"Come on, Ray! Move!" Carey screamed and Ray willed his muscles to rise and begin running.

Carey was in full sprint and Ray followed numbly. It seemed surreal, like a movie clip playing silently on the screen.

Was this really happening? Ray shook his head and forced his feet to a speed he hadn't known was possible. Still, it moved like slow motion as the world blurred around him.

"You're dead, cop!" The words rang out from across the street.

Ray followed Carey to the alley ahead. They raced through the opening and two more bullets whipped by, one so close Ray heard the pop and felt his hair parting near his right ear.

Feet pounded the sidewalk behind them. Three, maybe four sets.

Hearts thumping, Carey and Ray melted into the shadows—and Carey, his gun drawn, waited for the assailants to barge around the corner. Ray searched for cover. A large trashcan lay across from him with only scattered boxes on the left. One of two barely visible doorways seemed the only option. Ray banged against the door and searched for the handle.

It was boarded tight. They were trapped.

"What's the plan?" Ray whispered harshly. "We're trapped."

A gunman rounded the corner and fired wildly down the alley. He vanished as quickly as he appeared.

Ray dived for the concrete, rolling into the opening, his back against the door. When no more shots came, Ray cautiously glanced around for Carey.

"Are you hurt, Carey?"

Strong arms clamped down over his head and mouth. Ray straightened and threw himself into the brick wall, sending the attacker staggering back, then rolled and got to his feet. Two big men faced him.

Long serrated blades came out. The shorter man motioned for Ray to come forward and try his luck.

"What you got, old man?" The knifeman sneered.

Ray crouched, a strange calm coming over him. All panic dissipated. His brief self-defense classes rushed to his senses. It'd only been a couple days a few years back, but he relaxed, balled up his fists and took a fighting stance. If he looked serious enough maybe he could scare them.

"Are you kidding me?" the knifeman asked, gesturing at him to his buddy. His astonishment quickly turned to fury and he charged Ray.

Ray dodged the wild knife swipe and clapped his hand on the man's right ear as he went huffing by. The man yelped in pain and Ray kicked him crashing into the wall. A rush of anger poured into Ray's veins and gave him hope.

How dare they beat me? Shoot at an officer? Steal my daughter?!

Fueled with righteous anger, Ray turned to the other man as curses exploded behind him and howling in rage, the knifeman charged again.

Twice Ray's weight and ten times as evil, the crazed man would fight to the death now. Ray had only a moment to turn and duck the other man's blow before the second thundered into him, sending him to the ground and expelling his breath. Ray brought his knee up blindly and caught the man in the groin flinging the knife away. The second man launched himself on top of them with such strength it flattened Ray's lungs and simultaneously smashed his head into the asphalt.

Ray gasped and swiped the air, hitting nothing. Something was wrong with his head and there was the coppery taste of blood in his mouth. He couldn't breathe. Thick pillows of black began to swallow his mind.

It'd soon be over. The second man was pinning him calling for the knife. *You have to fight, Ray. Don't give in. Fight for Amber. For Carey.*

If only he could free an arm to poke the man's eyes.

Suddenly the pressure on his chest released and Ray heard metal smash flesh. Turning to the sound, Ray heard Carey speak.

"You okay, Ray? Say something, bro."

"Carey?"

"We've got to get out of here. This isn't over."

Stumbling to his feet Ray leaned against the wall and breathed. Two men lay on the ground while a third groaned somewhere nearby.

"What now?" Ray asked.

"Get down!"

Carey pushed Ray down and Ray followed his gaze to more men coming down the alley. Frozen in place his mind begged his body to move. Bullets flashed by again. Carey dropped to one knee and shot back. He dropped the front man but missed the second and then they were caught in a firestorm. Soon, Carey was knocked down like a bowling pin, and then Big George loomed in Ray's vision.

Roaring like a wild animal, George's hands snatched Ray's throat. His fat thumbs fastened like tongs, piercing into his skin and crushing with frightening authority. Ray felt his windpipe close and excruciating pain blinded him. Gasping again, he fought helplessly against the darkness seeping in.

Ray raised his leg to knee him and made weak contact, but George only laughed and squeezed harder. Life drained quietly from Ray and like a heavy, black fog the blackness began devouring him. As his life was being taken, he prayed. "Jesus, protect Amber. Take care of my wife . . ."

The will to live was slipping away. But he didn't fear. Instead, he released his desire to fight.

As death closed in, the pressure suddenly released and an instinctive gasp brought breath back. Ray felt his body falling and the pavement rushed up to him, stunning him back to his senses, the thought tumbled into his mind:

"I'm alive?"

Through the semi-darkness still crowding his vision, his bloody hands swiped his eyes. Summoning every ounce of remaining strength, Ray sat up and took in the scene.

Big George stared up at him from the red asphalt with expressionless eyes.

Scooting backward, Ray pressed into the wall, using it to rise on shaky legs.

Faint beams of sunlight cut through the semi-darkness casting a golden hue upon the alley. Another day was dawning.

"Carey?" Glancing around, Ray saw no one.

He pushed forward, careful to stay an arm's length from Big George who continued laying in awkward silence. Oblivious to potential danger, Ray scoured the alley for Carey. To his left about twenty feet away, Ray saw him. Hurrying over, a gut-wrenching fear gripped him. He was face down, a long, white carved knife handle protruded from his back. Ray rushed to his friend and gently put his ear to Carey's nose. He laid his fingers on the detective's throat and prayed for a pulse. A tremor of life, and relief soared into his heart.

Carey was alive. Barely. But alive.

"Police! Get your hands up. Step away from the body."

"Dispatch, this is Captain Switzer. The area is secured. Send a wagon and call the coroner. We're going to need bags."

Submitting, Ray again felt the sting of pavement as his body was laid prone and he was handcuffed and read his rights. Ray suspected he was in deep trouble. He had blood on his hands and there was at least one dead body within twenty feet of him. No witnesses to collaborate his story. Why hadn't he heard anything before? Now he could hear sirens and the dispatcher repeating information and voices of shopkeepers complaining about broken windows and damages. And the man who had saved him was being carted off like an injured football player.

Silently sitting on the sidewalk, Ray watched the police handcuff those members of the gang who could be roused and then gather around Big George's unmoving body.

160

"Think Mueller got him?"

"Yeah. If there was anyone who deserved it . . ."

"I hear you. Waste of flesh."

"Nobody gonna miss this big boy."

"No doubt."

Ray raised his head and called out, "Where'd they take Mueller?"

The young black female officer turned. "Who are you?"

"Ray Ellis. He saved my life."

"He's the girl's father." Captain Switzer pushed into the circle surrounding Ray and knelt. "You want to tell me what happened?"

"Please, how is Detective Carey doing?" Ray begged.

"On his way to the emergency room. Knife in the back." The captain considered him. "You a praying man?"

"Yes sir, I am."

"He could use it."

Bowing his head, Ray said, "He didn't have to help me."

"I didn't want him to," the captain said. "But he did. Must be pretty important to him."

Ray blinked up at him, his eyes misting over. "God, heal Carey. Save his life. Don't let him give it for me."

24

Since the shootout, Ray had wanted nothing more desperately than to be at the hospital by Carey's side.

Unfortunately, there were millions of questions and official forms to sign. Hospital protocol was one thing, but police regulations? Ray realized he was entering a new world of risk averse bureaucracy and potential liability. After receiving a medical clearance from the paramedics, he was told in no uncertain terms by the officers that his request to visit Carey would be denied, both now and later, and they would be going downtown to "get the facts straightened out" and reports filed.

He went along begrudgingly, distracted by his thoughts and amazed by how much he now felt for Carey. Just a few days and they were brothers. Why hadn't he thanked him while he had the chance? Or even told him how much Carey's partnership had meant to him.

Would it have felt too weird?

Thought I'd learned my lesson about speaking up while I had the chance, Ray thought. But you couldn't assume there was time for that later.

He walked through the police station chiding himself. *A day late and a dollar short again, Ellis.*

A couple of hours later, Ray signed some final forms, gave his official statement and was released. Hailing a taxi, he immediately headed for Saint Mary's Hospital with prayers on his heart, a lump on his head and several new bruises on his body.

Still, he was alive. He must get in to see Detective Carey. Then find Amber.

At the precinct, he was told that within hours, the police would round up the remaining members of Big George's gang. Subsequent raids would garner illegal contraband of guns, drugs and stolen property. All additional information would be obtained regarding the prostitution ring and in no time, Big George's legacy would be dissolved.

"Does that mean we'll find Amber, my daughter?" Ray asked, trying to stay out of the way amidst the bustle in the office.

"That's what this was about?" The questioning officer sighed and looked up at him. Ray thought he saw a glimmer of sympathy. "Was Big George her pimp?" the short officer said, turning her attention back to the computer.

"I don't know," Ray said.

Chicago PD procedure was to bring in all women associated with a known pimp. Once all questions had been finally answered, Ray hurried to the county hospital. Had he stayed to see it, he would have been shocked by the array of women brought in—all ages, sizes, colors and types filed into the precinct for booking. Each were questioned and released as fast as they were processed.

An official record was filed but as everyone knew, beyond the law, the significance of individual lives mattered little.

And even Ray knew that without support, money or a place to live, most of the women and girls would only wind up hustling for someone else. Eager for their next fix and a means of survival, they'd return to continue the same sad cycle.

———·-

Tall and stark, the door to Detective Carey's hospital room stood slightly ajar, partially open. Uncertain about knocking, Ray did anyway and stuck his head in.

What do you say to the man who was shot, beaten and given multiple wounds for you? How do you convey your gratitude to a man who saved your life not once, but twice?

"Carey?" Now that he was here, what words could express how he felt for this guy he'd only known for a few days, but who was willing to lay down his life for a friend?

Summoning his fortitude, Ray brushed open the door and walked to Carey's bedside.

"Hi, Carey," Ray breathed softly.

"Ray?"

"Yeah."

"Good to see you." Carey pushed through half-open teeth, the air escaping through his lips with strain.

Ray inhaled sharply. "No. It's good to see you. How you feeling?"

"I've seen better days. But hey. I'm alive."

"Thank God for that."

"I was worried sick man. They wouldn't tell me anything."

Carey shifted to sit up. "I'll make it. Listen," He rolled his head to look at Ray. "Did you find Amber?"

"Not yet. Had a small problem with a pair of handcuffs."

"What? Let me make a call."

Ray held up a hand. "No. If she was part of the ring, they'll find her. If not, I will. But I've got to say something . . ." He looked at his hands, mustering his courage.

Suddenly, a phone began buzzing. "Sorry," Carey said, glancing under the sheets and grinning. "I hid it from the Nazi nurses." Ray blinked. "It's Captain Switzer," Carey said.

Ray nodded. "Do your thing."

"Captain." Carey squinted and seemed to wince. "Well, I'm still answering my calls, aren't I?"

Ray smiled.

"Yeah. He's here." Carey listened for a while. "I don't understand. You have her?" He covered the phone and mouthed the word to Ray.

Amber.

The suspense was killing Ray. What was going on?

"Well, how can they not know?"

Carey glanced at Ray. His eyes suddenly fell. "Oh. I see."

"What?" Ray blurted.

Holding his hand up, Carey sighed long. "Will do, Cap." Casting a glance out the small window, he waited. "Thank you, sir."

Sliding the cell phone back under the sheet, Carey took a moment to look at Ray.

"You need to go back to the precinct. You need to identify some-one they found." Carey swallowed. "They think she was your daughter."

"What? No." Ray couldn't believe it. He wouldn't. Anger and sadness wrestled for dominance in his chest.

"I don't know any details and they don't have many. I'm sorry, Ray."

"I don't believe it," Ray said, standing. *After all this?*

"There's no confirmation—" Carey offered.

Turning, Ray stumbled for the door. All other thought had fled and tears of fear came rushing from his eyes. He raced for the car, whimpering like a child fleeing a violent storm. Whether death or life awaited him, he could not surmise.

Still, he continued running.

Amber had been wandering the streets all night.

She needed money. She knew what to do to get it, but refused to follow that rabbit trail. This much she knew, her father was supposedly in Chicago and was looking for her.

It staggered her mind, and yet it brought deep, deep fear. Fear could be suffocating at times, and she hadn't felt this kind for several years. Maybe ever.

Every so often she would stop and gasp for breath.

What if I call him? What if he hates me? What if he takes one good look and walks away?

Her friend Leticia had said, "If my Dad showed up, I'd run. No way I would let that piece of scum touch me again."

I'm not his little girl anymore. I'm a druggie and a prostitute. I can't go back. It'll be easier for everyone if I just disappeared.

She saw the lights before she heard the din emitting from Big George's hangout. Twirling squad lights and flickering emergency flashers brightened the dull, sodden air of the southern sky. Like a creature fixated on the blur of color and sound, Amber trudged closer and closer to the corner. Oblivious to her surroundings she plunged headlong into the commotion and noise of the annihilation of Big George's operation.

"Hey, I think she's one of them," yelled an officer.

"Yep. Arrest her."

She tried to run, but strong hands grabbed her, causing a shrill cry to escape.

"Easy, girl."

"What's your name?" an officer with a notepad asked without looking at her.

"It's over, honey," said another female officer.

"What's over?"

"You're coming downtown with us. And if you play your cards right, you'll never have to work the street again."

"What are you talking about?" Amber asked.

"Didn't you hear?"

"He's dead."

"What? Who is?" For a moment, she imagined her father's face.

"Big George, honey." Seeing the shock on her face, the officer nodded. "Dead as a doornail."

———

Speeding anywhere in Chicago was begging for trouble but careening into a police station at insane speeds not only looked but seemed like suicide. Yet there he was driving like a crazed mad man hell bent on finding the truth about his daughter. His mind numbed with fear, Ray stumbled into the lobby and demanded someone tell him what was going on.

The pale gray clock on the wall skipped a notch and Ray realized he was staring like a bloodthirsty zombie at the clock as if it held the answer to the question pounding in his head.

Was Amber alive?

"Ray Ellis?"

"Yes."

"Come with me."

"I'm sorry, I don't understand—"

"Please come with me. I'll explain everything."

Moments later Ray was ushered into a small room with nothing more than a table and two chairs. A plate glass window lined the far wall, but otherwise the walls were blank and devoid of color with dingy white paint that flaked and peeled.

What is this? Ray wondered. *A scene from Blue Bloods?*

Seconds later a female police officer walked through the door.

"Mr. Ellis I'm sorry for the delay."

Wanting to shout the words he managed a blubbery question.

"Is she dead? Is my Amber . . ."

"I'm so sorry Mr. Ellis. There's been a horrible mistake. We found a dead girl and one of George's girls thought her real name was Amber."

Pausing, she continued. "But she was mistaken and again we apologize for the stress I know this has put you through."

"Wait. You're saying there's been a mistake? How? How can someone screw up something this important?"

"I'm sorry. That's all I know to tell you. It's just been a terrible misunderstanding. Please wait right here."

Turning abruptly she slid through the door and disappeared. Ray closed his eyes and prayed like he had never prayed before.

"Mr. Ellis."

And stepping aside she ushered in the young lady tagging behind her.

"Yes."

"Is this your daughter?"

Ray stumbled to his feet and then tripped over a protruding chair as he walked toward Amber.

Stopping in front of her, his eyes gazed at a woman he did not know, but a child he had loved dearly. Amber looked at Ray, her eyes frozen open in shock and disbelief. Ray swiftly glanced at the officer standing by and asked, "Can we talk?"

"Sure go ahead," she motioned stepping back a couple of feet. Implied but not spoken was that Amber was still in her custody.

"I'm sorry, Amber." Ray haltingly began. "If I could do it over . . ."

Amber heard, but they registered no meaning. All she saw was the man she had called "Daddy." In an instant, she broke and Ray watched stunned and amazed as she moved toward him. The wall of misunderstanding that had been built between them these past six years came tumbling down in a millisecond. Love had not disappeared; it was only hidden by distance.

Nothing prepared them for the tears that would not be contained. As the stones fell, the moment seemed to plunge into eternity. The slow drip of their tears cascaded faster and faster until finally the wall burst open and the torrent plummeted unchecked down their cheeks as he held her like he'd never let go.

———

Amber came to him. Easing her arms around his waist she pressed her head to his chest and let the sobs have their way. Ray could not find breath. A sense of euphoria gripped his body. She was in his arms. His daughter had been found. Ray slid his arms around her back and hugged her tight. He, too, was weeping.

As Ray held Amber he sensed that while he might be holding the body of his twenty-year old daughter, the soul and mind of his fourteen-year old forgotten, abandoned child was actually in his embrace.

No hug, tear or kiss could change the life of Amber. Nothing would ever replace those lost moments.

For now, they held each other. That was enough. This was everything.

25

"Carey, I've got someone for you to meet."

"What?"

Ray walked quickly to the door and disappeared into the hallway. Seconds later his head poked back into the room. "Detective Carey. Meet my daughter, Amber Ellis."

Carey's eyes glistened and he said, "It's nice to meet you, Amber."

"It's nice to meet you, Detective." Amber inched toward the bed.

"Please, call me Carey," and extending his hand he waited for her response.

Like old friends catching up at a school reunion, laughter and joy soon echoed in the small hospital room. For each, pain had no voice, and abuse and neglect were vanquished. Once complete strangers with only a common quest they now revealed themselves and welcomed friendship into their hearts.

About twenty minutes later a soft knock landed on the door and a medical technician walked into Carey's room.

"Hi, I need to check our patient. Would you guys like to wait outside?"

"Oh no problem, we need to get going," Ray offered.

"Okay, I'll give you a moment."

"It's nice to have met you Amber," Carey said once again extending his hand for Amber to shake.

Grabbing his hand she leaned in and lightly kissed him on the forehead. Breathing the words barely above a decibel she whispered.

"Thank you, Carey. You saved me. I'll never forget you."

"No, thank you, Amber. You saved me."

Seeing the puzzled look on Amber's face, Carey quickly added. "I'm so glad to have met you and your father."

"Give me a minute, Amber-Lamb?" Ray asked.

"Sure, Dad."

Ray studied his shoes. "What can I say? Thanks for stepping out into the deep end with me man. Thank you."

"And thank you, Ray."

"No . . ." Ray protested.

"No, I'm serious. To see you and your daughter together . . ." Carey's remaining words were choked off as he swallowed hard and turned his head to stare at out the window.

"Stay in touch."

"We will. We will."

The replay would later wash over Carey as without distinction he saw an angry man sitting alone in his squad car, wondering if he could save just one. And if so, would it be worth it?

Etched permanently into Carey's mind, he knew it would sink perceptibly deep into his heart, that moment when the answer to his question was answered emphatically with a resounding big sloppy, "Yes."

Yes, it was worth saving one. And that one could become more. And he would keep trying. Because if all he could do was save one, then his life was not in vain. He would have fulfilled a sense of purpose, a higher calling to move out of his "first world" mind-set, which too obsessively thought only of himself. And finally, he would glimpse a view of the world. A world not devoid of hope and love but formed with hope and restoration.

———--

Walking to the door, Ray glanced back at Carey and offered a weak goodbye. Stumbling into the hallway, he saw his daughter and without warning, she grabbed his hand. Squeezing tight, she looked at Ray and said.

"I'm just so glad to meet a good man, Daddy."

Fighting for control of his emotions, he replied.

"Yes. He is."

And again as if to emphasize and add deeper meaning to his thoughts, he repeated.

"Yes, he is."

———--

Amber scooted into the booth seat and radiantly smiled at Rachel.
"Hi."
"Amber, it's great to see you."
"Are Jayhawk blue and red your colors?"

Amber made a puzzled face.

Casually flipping her scarf across the table she shyly said, "I want you to have this. And . . ." pausing to slow her racing pulse she finished. "Maybe you won't forget me."

Fighting tears, Amber firmly said, "I'll never forget you. Never. You helped me when I had no hope."

"So. Going back home?" Rachel intoned.

Amber nodded. "Dad and Mom need me," and a faint smile flashed on her face. "And maybe I need them to."

They both laughed, a strange sound to Amber's ears. It was not the hollow thump of pain and nausea they had shared so recently.

"You got my number." Amber said.

"You know I'll use it."

Fixing her gaze squarely on Rachel, Amber shifted. "We'll stay friends?"

Without blinking, Rachel smiled. "More than that. Sisters. Sisters for life."

26.

Glancing in his rear view mirror, Ray glimpsed the silly grin plastered across his face.

Yep. There was no mistaking it. The joy in his heart was painted across his face.

He knew he'd have to reintroduce Amber to folks. But now he wondered if they would recognize *him.*

He was a changed man. The whiskered, hollow-eyed person had stayed back in South Chicago. A full new hope had reconfigured his countenance and his heart was singing a song it hadn't recalled for years.

Pulling the mirror down, he looked in the back seat where Amber slept. "My Amber-lamb," he whispered. "I found you." He felt the tears again. "I can't believe I found you."

The gray skyline of Chicago eroded into the dusky sky. As the miles fell behind them, the emotion of Ray's last phone call with his wife Amanda brazenly surged through his mind. The memory still so fresh he could taste it.

———

Amber was awake and wanted food. "Your choice!" Ray had excitedly proclaimed.

"Its just lunch Daddy." Amber's patronized.

"I know but it's my first lunch with . . ." and a lump formed in his throat and he could not finish.

"Let's get Chinese. I miss Auntie Chin."

"Chinese it is."

"Your mom is blowing up my phone. I need to call her."

Amber was silent and continued stuffing down noodles and orange chicken.

"Amanda, it's Ray."

She'd sighed. "It's late Ray. Why didn't you call earlier?"

"I found Amber. She is right here with me."

Silence.

"Amanda?"

"Ray." Her voice was flat and cold. It threw him. "You will not keep hurting me." Her tone was laced with anger. Ray was stunned but he had the truth on his side. He pressed forward.

"I love you, Amanda. I would never joke about this. Never." He heard a gasp and plunged on. "I found her in Chicago. She is right here. Safe. With me." He handed Amber the phone. "Say hello to your mother."

"Mom? It's me. Amber." She'd stifled a sob. "I'm sorry."

Sliding the phone across the table, she covered her mouth, shook her head and escaped to the restroom.

At first, Ray thought Amanda had hung up. But when he held the phone to his ear, he knew she was there and something had shifted.

"Amanda. It's me again."

He said nothing else. Just listened. He mashed his ear to the speaker, senses heightened with attention. Was she crying? The quiet was deafening.

Did she believe?

If she did, the simplest words could speak life.

Ray had believed. And he had believed for Amanda as well. She, too, would know this unspeakable joy.

A sob. *There!* He heard it again. He was certain. Her cries of pain crossed through the telephone lines and gripped his heart. His breath shuddered and his hands clenched the phone so tightly he feared it might break.

"Amanda?" His voice was choked. "Amanda. Are you there?"

Was he imagining it? Again, this time, a stifled wail, the sound of a broken-hearted mother weeping from the depths of her soul.

Ray ached with her and waited, but his spirit soared and he gave thanks to God.

Darkness had to flee. Oh, my Savior God, to thee we lift our praise.

Ray whispered. "I'm here, Amanda. I love you. Thank you, Jesus." He desperately hoped for some word that would comfort his broken wife. Finally, after a long time, Amanda spoke.

"I'm so sorry!" cried Amanda. "My baby! Ray, please bring her home."

"Yes." He choked for air. "Yes, I promise."

"Oh Ray." Amanda wailed again, freer this time and the world seemed to tilt onto its axis as Ray felt something in him crash. Yet within moments, she seemed to collect herself. "Ray, thank you. Thank you. Thank you . . ." Her voice trailed off into sobs.

Fighting for control a slight cry emitted from his throat, uncontrolled, but not denied. His voice breaking from the emotion he said, "She is one hurtin' girl. She needs her mama." He sniffed and wiped his eyes. "We'll be home tomorrow morning. I'll call along the way. I have so much to tell you. And Amanda?" Gathering his courage, Ray pushed on. "Can I ask you a favor?"

Hearing nothing he struggled on.

"Meet us at the house? You and the kids?"

"Okay." More quiet sniffles. Then finally, "Come home, Ray. Just . . . let's all come home."

Hope rushed like water into Ray's chest and his heart leaped.

"And Ray?"

"Yes."

There was only one thing left to say. One phrase he'd hardly expected, but the words once spoken, he'd forever cherish. Because they were the ones in his own heart.

"I love you."

"I love you too, babe."

Pictures of fish, horses and oranges stared at Ray as he closed the phone, laid it on the table and slowly slid down the booth seat. Hands in his head, had anyone been around, they would have seen a grown man blubbering like a toddler.

The timeless years of torment, the interminable agony of their loss, and the unremitting insanity of trying to hold it together, it all fell and crumbled around him. Lost in the tall grass, Ray bellowed like a calf for its mother. The revelation of new life, of love lost and found again, and unspeakable pain now slowly ending, had struck with a force few men would ever know.

And now, he had weathered even that.

———

Amber looked back one last time at her apartment through the old truck window. She'd said goodbye to a few girls while gathering

178

her few things and she'd given her Bible to one of them. They'd exchanged numbers and promised to stay in touch. Dad had stayed in the car.

She turned to him. "It's so hard. Knowing those girls will probably return to prostitution."

He didn't answer for several moments. "I'd even help with a place to stay if they'd just get help and sign up for a job placement program. Or something." He looked at her. "But would they?"

"Probably not," Amber said. "They can't understand anyone caring."

They rode in silence for a while.

They passed all her familiar haunts, the years seeming to blend together in a swirling dust cloud floating off the plains. "Dad, I need to make one quick stop."

"We need to get on the road."

She pleaded. "It's important to me, Dad."

A smile crept over his face. "You always knew my weak spot. Where to?"

"Auntie Chin's."

"I should have known."

They wound their way down E Street. Amber saw a city desert, cold and soulless. Old lyrics came back to her. *Why so long to know you were so wrong, when you knew it held nothing?* Relief washed over her. The nightmare was finally over.

Outside the city, she thought. *There's a light in his face. He opens the door and welcomes you to his place. He asks you where you've been. You tell him who you've seen. You talk about everything. He saves your life.*

"Thank you, Jesus," she whispered.

Roused from his musing, Ray echoed the sentiment.

"Thank you, Jesus."

They arrived and Ray parked out front.

"I'll only be a couple minutes," Amber said, entering the small shop. Auntie Chin was stacking cans of oysters on a shelf.

"Hi, Auntie Chin."

"Child! You beautiful. You get haircut? Or just find way home?" She stood to her full height, her grin as infectious as ever.

Laughing, Auntie Chin went to her and wrapped her arms around her and squeezed hard.

Amber cried.

"You strong. Drink strong coffee?" she asked.

"Hee-hee!" Auntie Chin laughed and flexing her wiry arms, she struck a pose to demonstrate her might. Amber laughed too, but this mysterious woman she called friend was that strong. And more.

Auntie Chin's hands fastened onto Amber arms, and locking eyes she asked, "You go home with father?"

Amber nodded and Auntie Chin frowned as tears streamed down Amber's face. Still nodding, she buried her face into Auntie Chin's chest. "Oh, I'll miss you Auntie Chin," she said, wiping her eyes. "I'll miss you a lot."

"Child," Auntie Chin said, patting her head. "I see you again. Maybe here, maybe heaven."

Amber recovered and stood, still nodding and wiping her eyes. She caught a laugh. "I'll always remember you like this. With my tears on your apron."

Auntie Chin looked down. "This okay. I save tears for you till you come back."

She reached down and grabbed two cans of oysters. "One for you, one for father."

Amber smiled, took them, and gave her one final hug. "Thank you. For everything."

"You welcome, child. I learn a lot from you, too."

———

Amber climbed into the back seat of the truck. "I'm tired, Daddy. I think I'll sleep."

"Sure, Amber-lamb." He caught himself. "Sorry. Is it okay if I call you that?"

"Of course, Daddy. Always."

Smiling, she slid down, fluffed her pillow, and pulled her blanket around her.

She listened to the radio play a country western song. She closed her eyes. *"Cold on the outside but warming on the inside. All I want to know is how tomorrow is going to feel."*

"For sure." Amber said to herself. "For sure."

———

Amber could not feel the wind but the evidence of its existence spread visibly before her as stalks of grain waved peacefully across the open plain. Aware of her surroundings Amber slipped once more into the world of her dreams. She knew she was dreaming. But, she was home and it felt good to return to a place of beautiful memories, quiet conversations, and complete happiness.

"Jesus." She called.

"Hey, Amber. So. This is it?"

"Yep. I'm going home."

"I'm so happy for you, Amber." His gaze fastened upon her. "So happy."

Abruptly, a deep sense of panic seized Amber. Glancing into his face the awareness shook her and instantaneously she understood. Uttering the words forced her to a new courage. Avoiding

181

engagement, she could barely speak the thought thrusting itself upon her.

"You're leaving aren't you?"

"Yes. Amber. I am. But not like you think."

"But why?"

"I don't understand."

"Why are you going? I need you. I don't know what to do next." She gushed quickly.

"I know. And you will always have me. It's up to you to live your life, but I will show you what to do." Jesus answered.

And as if to answer her fears, he continued. "Remember what I said in John chapter 14?"

Without waiting for her reply, he quoted, *"Do not let your hearts be troubled. Trust in God; trust also in me. In my Father's house are many rooms; if it were not so, I would have told you. I am going there to prepare a place for you. And if I go and prepare a place for you, I will come back and take you to be with me that you also may be where I am. You know the way to the place where I am going."*

"And you know what Thomas one of my disciples said?"

Amber set her chin and straightened. "No. I don't recall."

"'Lord, we don't know where you are going, so how can we know the way?' So I told him, 'I am the way the truth and the life. No one comes to the Father except through me.'"

The words of Jesus sparkled like diamonds on a black velvet cloth. The contrast illuminated their significance. The dark cloth was his last testament to the disciples and now, to Amber. In a short while the world she knew was going to collapse into even more unbeliev-able chaos. Yes, she would be safe, but would once again experience new pain and hurt. The pain of lost years with her family would sting her new reality and even though love would envelop her from much, new hurts of rejection and disdain would mar her new world.

"That's always been the question, Amber. *'Lord where are you going?'*"

Jesus was silent, and Amber, thoughts flickering, slowly said, "Jesus?"

Turning his head he gently looked at Amber.

Her voice quivered. "Why can't I go with you? Why do I have to wait?"

"It's not your time, Amber. You have much to see and experience first. You will be like a diamond on a black cloth. You will shine against the backdrop of this world and illuminate my love and forgiveness to many. Don't let your heart be troubled."

Amber cried.

"I know you," Jesus continued. "I know you are so easily alarmed. And it appears you are surrounded by seemingly disastrous possibilities. I see your heart, just as I saw the disciples'. I know what you are thinking. But my heart is big. So big that I have room for all the troubles of your life."

Pausing for breath, Jesus plunged on, the determination in his voice and spirit consuming Amber like a raging fire surging forward.

"But here's the secret of strength. *'Trust in God; trust also in me.'*"

Listening intently Amber blurted out, "But what does trust mean? I mean. Really mean?"

"That's a fair question, Amber." Cocking his head slightly, his eyes squinted, and Jesus sighed. "Well. I guess it's about continual faith. Believing, even though I won't be visible anymore. Believing in me even when it seems like I've abandoned you—which I haven't. When I was headed to the cross, it looked as though all my words were about to be proved false. Everyone's hope in me was about to be dashed."

He stood taller. "Things are going to happen that will cause you to doubt me. You might think I have deserted you. But just as you believe in God even though you don't see Him . . . believe also in me."

He looked so softly at her. "Amber, I am asking you to leave the safety of this cocoon and venture into unfamiliar territory. New and different things are always frightening."

The care of Jesus' words seeped into Amber's heart and she ventured a reply. "I want to trust you, and to trust you have a plan for my future."

Standing motionless Amber stared into the horizon. Her heart was heavy, but she could not let him go without saying this. "Thank you for helping my Dad find me. I know it was you."

He smiled. "Your dad's determination and Carey's friendship were not merely my doing. Their willingness to listen and risk was astounding."

He took her hands. "There are good men in this world, Amber. Many don't know their own self-worth or strength at times, all they've known is the pain of feeling powerless. And it has rendered them helpless. Some only need the nudge of a loving woman, someone like you, to find their heroic hearts. Make room for the one I send. And you will find healing."

Dropping her hands, he gently placed his hand on her head. "Father, give Amber the Counselor to guide and quicken her each day to live in truth and hope. Help her to remember that I will never leave her or forsake her. Remind her that my spirit lives in her."

He removed his hand and smiled. "Look and watch for me! I love you, my daughter. Forever."

Opening her eyes, Amber blinked but he was already gone. Like warm snow melting into the frozen earth, in a wisp, he'd vanished.

27

Ray had noticed before of course, how distance and space tends to be exaggerated on the wide-open plains. But he hadn't experienced it, the reality of it like this for several years. Maybe never.

What appears close in Kansas can in reality be miles away.

Tiny lights shined through the darkness that had fallen upon the horizon and in one place, the place they were heading, a strange luminous glow persisted. Though the specific reason for it was still unknown, somehow it was familiar to Ray's weary eyes.

And it brought peace.

"What is that Daddy?" Amber's voice trembled with fear.

"I'm . . . not sure, honey."

"Is it coming from our farm?"

"Nothing to be concerned about. Almost home now."

Biting his lip, Ray swallowed hard. Actually, he wasn't so sure himself what was going on, but he wanted to be strong for

Amber. It wasn't a fire, the light was bright. There was no reason for fear.

It grew brighter as they approached. Turning down the driveway to the farm, Ray's heart quickened and he tightened his grip on the steering wheel.

"I'm coming up front," Amber said as she slid over the console and plopped into the passenger seat.

In the headlights of the truck, Ray recognized the first couple standing with candles at the side of the long driveway. A line of people stood behind them lining the road. Ray slowed and Amber looked in amazement at the hundreds of people each holding candles all around and in front of and circling the house.

The memory crashed into Ray, six years ago as people stood in support after Amber had been kidnapped. They were back again now, remembering her, inviting her back, all of them here to welcome her home.

The lost had been found. She was home.

Amber's hands covered her mouth. "I don't understand. Is this for me?"

"I believe so."

"Oh, Daddy . . ."

"It's okay."

"I can't."

"Don't worry. They understand. We're getting you home."

True to Ray's words, people nodded and watched them pass, then silently walked to their cars. There would be time for welcomes and hugs later. But for now, they allowed her, her homecoming, happy to commemorate the event and then to slip away into the night.

Ray rolled the truck into the carport stall beside the barn and quietly turned off the engine. The people were all leaving, climbing into their cars as he was climbing out. He waved and walked around the front of the truck and opened Amber's door. Quietly he laid his hands upon Amber's shoulders. "Don't worry. It's going to be alright. Everyone loves you."

Amber's silence quickened a fear in Ray. A fear that maybe Amanda and the kids would be guarded and too cautious—it could be so easy to hurt her. He hadn't thought of it before, but the pain of a second abandonment could strike and wrap itself around her heart, pulling her into despair again. It was a deep-seated fear and simply knowing it existed would not stop its ugly stalking. He watched helplessly as it slipped around him constricting like a snake.

Ray shook it off, steeling himself. If they needed, he'd guide them in welcoming her. He didn't really think they would, but a little extra patience would probably be necessary.

Her hands were trembling and he took them in his. "I'll be right here with you."

Offering a quick prayer, he moved aside to let her out and he went to the back door and motioned for her.

Suddenly the door opened and Amanda, Eric and Grace stood before them and they saw him and then her.

Amber stopped, standing in front of the truck.

Later he'd think how strange the situation really was. The kids ran to her—Eric and Grace—they had embraced her and probably seemed more at ease with the whole situation than he or Amanda. He had briefly spoken to both of them and they were so excited. "Amber will be back in the family, Dad," Eric had said, disbelieving. But in that moment he saw them not for himself, but for Amber. Each of them was beautiful, their eyes radiant and etched upon each face was both shock and disbelief. The reactions perfectly captured each of their personalities.

Amanda held herself up at the doorway, taking in the moment. Moisture pooled in her eyes. Tenaciously fighting for composure, the tears hung till they streamed down her cheeks and did not stop. They hugged and turned to her, mesmerized by her tears. No one spoke. A deep sustaining silence filled the low lit space between the truck and the backdoor.

Ray found himself struggling to even breathe as Amanda maintained her silent vigil. An eternity seemed to pass. Finally, Amanda fought loose and broke from the doorway, her shoes crunching the deafening silence.

She fell to her knees before reaching Amber and cried out.

"Forgive me, Amber! I lost my hope."

Her voice trailed off and was replaced by racking, anguished cries that broke Ray apart. Like a sledgehammer to the thin walls around his heart, her cries released the torment of the broken years and breathed hope into him again.

No one had ever truly forgotten.

Amber cried silently, walking toward her mother with outstretched arms. Kneeling, she grasped her mother's hands and looked in her eyes.

Pulling her to her feet, she hugged her. "I love you, Mom. Jesus forgives us all. And we are healed."

Sobbing with her, Amber pulled her mother close. Ray motioned for Eric and Grace to join them and they formed a circle, holding each other as they cried, laughed and breathed as a family.

Fear was gone. Love was back in the Ellis family.

In a couple of days, as they walked the fields together, Amber would tell him what she finally understood. In the end, far too many die alone. She'd seen it. Choosing to believe their cage is freedom, life eludes them even though they walk and talk and seem like you and me. Misery is their company. The finality of death is their only certain hope. Seeking their fortunes, they pine for tiny morsels of power. Insecurity and arrogance relentlessly stalk them until their final breath. And in those last sighs of life, the realization of dying alone stills the heart and rips the final gasps of existence from abandoned flesh. Amber understood because she too had lived in that empty space of existence.

But now, she said, taking his hand, she would walk no more in this sepulchre of death.

28
One Year Later

Though its name had changed several times, Gilroy Christian Center had existed for more than fifty years. As the years rolled by and times changed, the little church did its best to stay modern without sacrificing the message that God's love was for all.

Ray smiled at himself in the mirror as he got ready, feeling blessed that his children loved attending his childhood church. Their community was unique and their heartfelt care for them went beyond what he'd ever expected.

From the start, the church had lovingly welcomed Amber back and hope once again filled his and Amanda's hearts.

Yet today, expectations were running high.

By no small miracle they slipped in just as worship ended and Pastor Tommy stepped to the pulpit. "Welcome church! Today is a very special day as we prepare and commission Hope Home, the Ellis family's new mission project. I have permission from Amber to share a few details. As you might expect, a certain level of discretion and security must accompany this type of ministry, but we are excited to announce that Hope Home has secured downtown space on E Street in Chicago and will open in the next sixty days. As an extension of our church we are sending the Ellis family off to Chicago to begin their journey as inner city missionaries to those trapped by the streets and held by sexual exploitation. We are so proud of the work they have already done and the new work they are beginning soon."

Ray looked down the aisle to Amber. The sincere joy shone on her face and Ray was mesmerized by it, the beauty of it. She sat straight, her eyes wide and unblinking, and the slightest crease of a smile played across her lips.

How had he gotten so lucky?

Luck had nothing to do with it.

"It's been such an honor to join with them in this ministry," Tommy was saying. "And they've expressed to me their gratitude to all of you for your generosity and support."

Tommy's glance fell upon the Ellis family. "Let me tell you a story."

Looking around Ray saw cell phones go black, backs straighten, and heads rise. *"Ah, the power of a good story,"* Ray thought.

"Morning sun awakens the ancient mid-eastern village. It's another day like yesterday for the many vendors and shops that have been there for generations. The dirt street is filled with the jostling crowd that's come from far away to buy and sell. The sights and sounds of the early morning are mesmerizing. Your eyes, ears and nose come alive as the animals and carts pass by."

"Lying before you, your gaze fixes on treasures: exquisite handmade woodcarvings, weavings, cut stone, brass and silverworks. Suddenly, a sharp breeze wafts through and you hear the high tinkle of chimes. The air stills and you search for the sound, the shop of the village potter. You've heard rumors of his lovely pottery. Entering his shop, you find the aged man at a bench, stooped shoulders and a deeply creased face. It's dark inside and your eyes have to adjust. He continues his work until his newest creation is complete and he smiles and invites you to examine his work."

Ray looked over the faces in the audience. Everyone was in that shop.

"From simple lumps of clay, his hands craft his wondrous intentions, designing useful and magnificent masterpieces. Then, like a memory coming back, you know who this master is. You look up, but he has already realized he recognizes you. You are who he's been waiting for. He approaches you and even in the low light, you can see only the tenderness, the hope in his eyes.

"This man, he's known you and watched over you for a very long time."

The words cascaded through Amber's mind and a single tear slid slowly down her cheek. Her mind went back to the field she'd imagined so many times, the hollow where she'd burrowed. And Jesus. She smiled remembering his cap. His tenderness. The hope in his eyes.

Glancing over, Ray saw the tear and immediately felt his own eyes well with moisture. What was she thinking about? He didn't dare ask for fear of losing it then and there, and he quickly turned back to Tommy.

"From Jeremiah eighteen, verse one," Tommy continued, "'This is the word that came to Jeremiah from the Lord: 'Go down to the potter's house, and there I will give you my message.'" Tommy paused, looking out at the expectant faces. "'Pay attention, Jeremiah,' the Lord says. "So I went down to the potter's house, and I saw him working at the wheel. But the pot he was shaping from the clay was marred in his hands; so the potter formed it into another pot, shaping it as seemed best to him."

Tommy looked up again. "Can't you see Jeremiah watching this master, seeing how he works and wondering what God is trying to tell him?"

Ray imagined it. He'd asked God that question not long ago, in downtown Chicago, wondering where God was and making his own best guesses. For a while there it had seemed nothing was working and like a clumsy oaf he'd only mangled things.

But God had prevailed. His purpose was fulfilled.

Amber could see it in her mind, feel it like it was really happening again, Jesus holding her in his arms. She was crying and all he kept telling her was, "I love you. I love you." She had been lost and she'd given up hope and mangled things. But now she knew that a broken and contrite heart was all he asked.

"Then the word of the Lord came to me: 'O house of Israel, can I not do with you as this potter does?' declares the Lord. 'Like clay in the hand of the potter, so are you in my hand, O house of Israel.'"

Amber blinked back the tears. The truth of the words was directed specifically at her.

Tommy continued. "So the old potter slowly shuffles to the back of the shop. He finds what he wanted and begins molding a lump of clay in his strong, skilled hands, pressing it into a round, smooth ball. He sits to spin it on the wheel. His concentration is focused on this single lump of clay. For him, there is no other task. His eye sees what the average cannot imagine. He sees it not in its current form as a lump of worthless clay but as it could be one day, a beautiful, purposeful vessel, a magnificent work of rare beauty."

Pastor Tommy paused again and turned to Amber. "Amber Ellis. Would you come and share a little of the magnificent work God's been forming out of your heart?"

As spontaneous applause rose, Ray sensed the unity that had always bound them together here.

Ray felt the squeeze of his wife's hand. Tears of love welled in her eyes and Ray crumbled.

Amber took the mic from Tommy. "Perfect love casts out fear," she began. "For many years, I lived in fear. But Jesus came and showed me perfect love. It is no coincidence we are all here today. He's got something great planned for each of you. For me. For us." Amber's eyes flashed across the big room, but Ray felt the words and understood.

"For us," she repeated.

Ray glanced at Amanda and returned the smile on her face. And tears fell like rain.

"What is truth?" Amber continued. "Have you thought that? I have. Truth is the power of love. And that's the only thing that can set you free from your pain. Your substitutes. Your shame."

Her head dropped and Ray saw she was fighting for composure. He silently breathed a prayer for strength.

"Here's what I know. If you eliminate the impossible, what's left, no matter how improbable, that is the truth." Her hands nervously shifted on the metal podium.

There's the million-dollar question, Ray thought: *What really is truth? And she's not only discovered it, she's living it.* He prayed everyone might know the truth Amber had discovered.

"There's a precise moment in life when the truth hits you and a new realization may penetrate your soul. There is no alternative, no holding back even one bit of yourself. You can only accept and obey. And finally the spirit breaks. It's in that break, that remorse and regret where God, through the power of the Holy Spirit, speaks. And suddenly all fear is vanquished. And in that moment we begin to become the masterpiece he created."

Amber struggled for breath but pushed on. "I know I'm free. Free from sin. Free from shame. And free to help others discover what Jesus taught me."

Ray's heart threatened to burst as Amber turned slightly and stared directly at her father and slowly raised her head.

"And I can say this with all confidence—" Her throat caught and she began sobbing, but still she rushed on. "I'm free! I'm free! I am free. And I thank my Jesus and my dad who lives for him and believes with me every day . . ." She sniffed and swiped at her free-flowing tears, setting down the mic and turning away from the podium. She raised her arms to heaven and bawled. "I am free indeed! Thank you, God! Thank you for letting me share your love!"

She knelt, burying her face in her hands and Ray was up, moving quickly to the stage. Murmurs of praise rose and others cried out but Ray could hear only one thing,

Free indeed. Free indeed.

He reached her and put his arm around her and she jumped to hug him. He led her down, half carrying, meeting Amanda at the bottom, all of them a happy wet mess of beautiful, holy tears.

Someone stood and clapped and as they walked back to their seats, thunderous applause rang out and everyone was on their feet, praising and worshiping together.

Others reached out and hugged them, patting her and thanking her for her words, each feeling their personal response to the truth she'd spoken.

They found their seats and Amber received hugs from her brother and sister as she sat. Ray had never known such a feeling of love and community in all his life.

Oh, that everyone might know the truth Amber had discovered.

Pastor Tommy took the stage again and after a few moments, he broke the hush that had descended, his voice ragged and choked. "This is what we have all waited for. This moment. This masterpiece. What is the Master Potter seeing in this work of his today? And what does he see for all of us within his unknowable purposes?"

He looked out over the faces, obviously saving the moment. "Will you bow your heads with me?"

He prayed for the Ellis family, for their ministry, and for the Master Potter to reform all of their lives into what he saw fit. A beautiful goblet or a peasant's bowl, he prayed they'd simply trust and be completely his.

Amber sniffed again and listened intently to Tommy's prayer. She thought of the families not represented, the families who still knew loss and those who hadn't been so lucky as her to be found yet.

She thanked God for her loving family. For the friends she'd made on her journey. Kena. Rachel. Detective Carey. Auntie Chin.

She prayed for her childhood family and friends. For all those who didn't yet know him like she did.

She prayed for courage and wisdom to share what she now knew—that even in the worst situations, there is hope and a love beyond all understanding. She prayed for Meghan.

Moments later, the church crowded the front, surrounding the Ellis family to commission them into service for Hope Home. As they prayed, Amber thought she glimpsed a vision, a brief scene she would later recall. A view of the place she was headed.

She couldn't hold back the tears when she felt them coming again. Eric handed her a tissue and they all held her tighter.

Here was her truth. This love that couldn't be contained.

No, Meghan might never be found, she thought.

But she would never, never stop searching.

Acknowledgments

To the many who toil deep into the night, to those who labor in dimly lit caves during daylight, to those who dig their toes in the beach while burning their flesh. To all those who with their thoughts and words make this world a better place, who give us hope, who help us seek redemption, I say thank you.

This list is not exhaustive but represent those who mark a man and challenge his soul.

To my science fiction and fantasy writers, I salute you. Isaac Asimov, Ray Bradbury, Frank Herbert, J.R.R. Tolkien, C.S. Lewis, Ted Dekker, and Madeline L'Engle. For my suspense and mystery side, I thank James Scott Bell, Jerry Jenkins, Stephen Bly, and Sigmund Brouwer. To Tosca Lee and Steven James, your work has challenged me both as a writer and reader.

Thanks to the Mt. Hermon Writers Conference for jumpstarting my path. To Neil Dunlop, James Scott Bell, Randal Langley,

Robert Curry, Jeff Howe, and countless friends who believe in me and have supported me.

Special thanks to Mick Silva, my editor, for without you, I would be a dead man. Your name should be on the cover.

I also wish to thank my Uncle Ed and Aunt Winnie, my wife, Chris, my children, Ashley and Wesley, my son-in-law, Devon Robeson, my sister, Beth, and her husband, Barry, for never doubting my ability. And to my granddaughter, Delaney, your precious life reveals the length and breadth of the measures one takes to save a loved one.

Love to all,
Dr. Lon W. Flippo

Reading Group Guide

1. There is a thin line between psychological and spiritual conflict. *Sepulchre* focuses on the battle in the mind and how the victory leads to spiritual understanding. Considering the emotional conflict Ray and Amber undergo, what might you say about this connection between the mental and the spiritual?

2. What obstacles did they encounter which could have derailed Amber and Ray in their journey toward hope and restoration? Have you overcome roadblocks to find spiritual hope?

3. Amber's and Ray's journeys elicit the help of Rachel and Carey. Why would others help when no easy solution seemed plausible?

4. In this story, characters blur across the lines as victim, rescuer, bystander and perpetrator. Which characters fall into those categories? Are the lines truly blurred?

5. Amber searched for Jesus Christ on her own out of her desperate need. Such passion can be inspiring but often our pursuit of him is less intense. What does your pursuit of faith look like?

6. Many people struggle with feeling God is harsh and severe, which makes them doubt he's molding them into anything good. Can you relate and how are you combating your unbelief?

7. Carey's selflessness propelled his mission to help Ray even to the point of risking his own life. Seeing sacrifice overcome selfishness here, did you believe that could happen in real life? What would it take?

8. Do you feel personally unaffected by human trafficking? Do you wonder what good anyone can do, much less what you could contribute? Would you pursue action if it was your daughter or sister?

Please visit these websites for information about contributing to end human trafficking in your community:

See A Dance for Bethany: humantraffickingmovie.com

Cwfa.org

state.gov/j/tip/id/help/

Polarisproject.org

humantraffickinged.com

endslaverynow.org

notforsalecampaign.org

humantrafficking.org

youthfortomorrow.org

www.projectrescue.com

LON FLIPPO has a doctorate of ministry from Assemblies of God Theological Seminary and pastored for over thirty years. He is currently a professor of Children and Family Ministries at North Central University in Minneapolis, MN. His work has received acclaim from readers for its realism and theological insight, parents looking to pass their faith on to children, and teens caught in the modern challenge of connecting scriptural wisdom to modern life. Find more at www.iParentnow.com (@iparentnow).